MISSISSIPPI DEEP

DAHLIA STORM

The Reading Glass Books
1-888-420-3050
www.readingglassbooks.com
production@readingglassbooks.com

Dedication

I dedicate my book to my family and friends.

Acknowledgment

I want to thank God and the universe for giving me another chance to fulfill my writing destiny. I am a miracle, and I'm grateful for all the unknown heroes among us.

I also want to thank Rosemary, my sprit friend. She had a touching story to tell about her family's survival during the depression. I would like to thank my family and friends for their encouragement.

Also, I would like to thank the Marvel ghost-writers team — Brad Miller, Oscar Thomas, and Ivana Lawrence — for their expertise. I will thank my fans in advance and welcome you into my world.

About the Author

As an author who had been hiding in a box for years, Sandra Smith had an awakening when someone from the other side contacted her. Little did she know that it was the beginning of something fulfilling – something exciting! The whole experience, although overwhelming, prompted her to write her first mystery thriller.

As Sandra delved further into the story of her spirit friend, she reached a dead-end with more unanswered questions than ever, but she never gave up. With this book, she aims to share her journey with the readers who inspired her to fulfill her writing destiny – once again!

Contents

Chapter One

The Paranormal

It had been four months since her husband's demise, but the pain was still afresh. No matter how hard she tried, she ended up at the end of the dark end of the vortex of her memories. The loneliness prevailed, and it had only become unbearable with time. Her mind was stuck in the past; she struggled to live in the present. Amidst the pain and distress, there was a longing for one last conversation or anything that could help her gain closure.

"Susan, what's for dinner?" his voice still echoed in her head when it was past 8 o'clock in the evening.

Following the death of her husband, she was initially in denial. The memories they had together were etched deep in her senses; she would lose track of what was real and what was just memories. She would sit alone for hours; Susan could only cry so many tears before she would drain herself emotionally all over again.

After her husband's funeral, Susan's friends and family returned to their lives, leaving Susan alone and lonely in the house. There was plenty of food lying on the table; Susan was hungry and decided to eat something. By this time, she had somewhat managed to comfort herself to some extent, but it would still take a long time for her to get over the trauma.

"Or maybe it is meant to be like this!" She was ready to spend the rest of her life with just his memories.

With her mind still stuck there, Susan decided to sort out the photos that were lying around in a drawer. It was a mere attempt to calm the chaos in her mind that was not letting her rest.

She sat on the carpeted floor and began sorting the old photographs. There were pictures of them, their children, and all the memories they made together. She also came across the old photographs of her father and mother in the family farmhouse that they had captured. Susan had spent a great time on that family farmhouse, and those photos opened the box of memories that she had long forgotten.

As she looked at those photos one by one, a shadow of loneliness hovered over her. The sight of her family farm reminded her of the get-togethers and late-night sittings with her loved ones. A part of her was craving to relive those moments for one more time, but she knew there was no way she could reignite the old magic or bring the lost ones back to life.

Susan sat in the same spot for a while; her mind was stuck somewhere as she struggled to make a decision. Suddenly, she got up with determination; she had not felt this energetic in a long time.

"The house needs renovation, and so does my life!" she thought to herself.

Recovering from the trauma of losing her husband, Susan finally decided to take baby steps toward life. She decided to go to the family farm because she needed to feel at home and safe. She got up and started getting ready for her solo trip, hoping it would take her back to the good old days.

***

It was raining as Susan drove on the Great River Road, and memories of vivid hues danced in front of her eyes. The glimpse of the Mississippi River filtered her thoughts with the images of a haunted burial ground, broken barges, old boats, garbage, and oil spills homing deep beneath the dark blue and swift water. In echo to the melody of the fall winds, the river was singing soulful blues. In the dark waters, thousands of sunken stories and truths flowed around the region, quenching earth and kin.

Spread across 1.2 million square miles, the Mississippi River was simply a sight to behold. It was the second longest river in North America, flowing from Lake Itasca through the center of the continental United States to the Gulf of Mexico. The scenic roadway reminisced the road trips she had with her parents.

The raindrops felt cold as her skin carried the heat of her blood; the pain was still fresh in her memories. As she strode onward, her eyes were desperate to find a rainbow that was promised by the light.

There was a dirt road that led Susan right to the farmhouse. A big yard marked the property's boundary, which belonged to her father. The leaves of the surrounding giant oak trees were painted in vibrant shades of orange and yellow.

In summer, Susan would spend hours looking at this beautiful view as the birds flew over her head, chirping to the song of the sunshine. A crispy sound would echo in the surroundings as she walked on the piles of dried leaves that would fall from the surrounding trees. But this time, it was raining.

After four months, she was finally out there trying to explore what the world had to offer. When she reached the destination, the farmhouse door was no less than a big, comfy hug upon return, a much-needed comfort Susan had been craving for all these months. It ensured the feeling, a great sense of having come home. The place had kept safe the memories of the good old times, the laughter, the countryside smell, and fading the painful events for a while.

The sound of her boot tapping on the wooden floor echoed in the void's silence as Susan wandered inside the empty house. The loud noise of thunder roared in the distance; Susan saw the raindrops sliding down the glass windows. It was getting chilly. Susan placed her bag on the wooden coffee table and sat down for a while.

"Oh no, I forgot it again!" she remembered the pending bills. Without wasting any moment, she took out her phone and got done with it. She sighed with relief as she leaned back on the chair.

Even the smallest tasks had become hectic lately, and she would feel mentally drained; it was overwhelming as she tried to figure out which bedroom she would make her own. She finally decided to go with her parent's bedroom, which had an attached bathroom. She struggled a bit to find clean linen; even though it smelled musky, she made peace with it.

As she snuggled into the big soft-feathered pillow, Susan could still hear the pattering of the rain on the old tin roof. She lay in bed for a while before falling asleep.

Thunder roared, and she felt as if the sky was about to break into two pieces. It was the darkest hour of the night. As lighting flashed from the sky, an image of the ruthless waters gushed against barges. There was a loud bang; perhaps it was the sound of a branch falling off the tree along with the debris. She stood there still, unable to breathe, when she witnessed a giant rock as tall as a mountain emerging from the dark water. The images of old sunken boats appeared in front of her eyes. The water did not spare anyone. The strong winds came thrusting onto her face, and she heard a voice amidst the chaos.

"Help me!"

It startled her for a second; she looked around, but no one was found.

"Help me!"

The voice was growing louder and louder.

"Help me!!"

Susan woke up with a jerk; her heart was racing as sweat gushed tricked down her forehead.

"What a dream it was!" she wondered.

It was not what she needed after a hectic day. Restlessness flew through her veins; she could not fall asleep after that. She grabbed her laptop and signed in to her social media.

Whenever she felt lonely, she browsed and scrolled her social media feed to catch up with her friends and family.

"That's all I do. Scroll and like!"

She smiled as she liked a heart-warming vacation picture of one of her friends.

As she scrolled down her newsfeed, an 'ad' suddenly popped on the screen.

Connect with your loved ones! The alphabet in bold read. **Psychics, Tarot Readings, Fortune Tellers.**

It was not the first time Susan had come across something like that. She had seen on TV that many people claimed to be clairvoyant with supernatural abilities to perceive events that are beyond normal sensory contact. Susan had never paid heed to such ads, but she was drawn toward it this time. She wanted to give it a try.

Not knowing what would come next, she clicked on the ad that led her to the psychic's website. She browsed a bit to find out more before submitting her application. It was exasperating at first with all the questions, but something inside her kept her going; it made her believe it was all true, and she didn't think twice before signing up for $50.

Once she had completed the form, she received a half fan with letters and a number on compliments of a psychic:

"It has all the answers to your questions."

Susan felt excited after a long time. She also got her tarot cards that were supposed to come in the mail, but she was able to download the fan online. It was similar to the Ouija board she had seen in the movies.

As she was trying to figure out how to go about the fan, she dozed off and woke up late the next morning. Finally, she had found something to keep her busy for a while; she decided to start the house's renovation. The drive to town was over an hour, and she could find a Lowe's store. She also ordered a dishwasher and kitchen sink, but she had to wait a couple of days for her order to arrive. She didn't mind because time was on her side.

On her arrival back home, a truck was pulling up in her yard. A tall, handsome man approached her car and introduced himself as James. He was her neighbor, and he lived a few miles down the road.

Susan was excited to know that she had a neighbor.

"Nice to meet you. You caught me returning from a Lowe's store where I just ordered some appliances for my house. I'll pick them up in a couple of days."

"I can help you with that," James replied when she told him about the renovations she had in my mind.

James was kind; Susan felt as if the stars were lining up. Before returning home, she gave him her number so he could give her a call when the supplies came in.

Coming back to the house, Susan felt proud of herself as it was a productive day. She grabbed her computer and leaned back in her dad's big, comfy chair. She opened her email, hoping that she would get to hear from her children, but there was none.

"They must be busy!"

Susan knew very well that her kids were busy in their lives, and she would try not to bother them. As she scrolled down the screen, sudden excitement rushed through her veins. There was a mail from the psychic website; she had just got her download for the fan.

"Let's do this!" she clicked on the email, smiling from ear to ear.

As she read the instructions in the email, she realized she needed a dowel to hold over the fan. The dowel was supposed to swing to letters on the fan to spell a word, or it would just point to yes or *no.*

"Ahan. That's interesting!" she said while grabbing her cross necklace as a dowel.

She was halfway through it when her phone rang. It was James.

"I will be at your house tomorrow at 8:00 in the morning to start the renovation," he informed politely. "So, put the coffee on!"

Susan smiled.

She was excited yet anxious to rebuild the kitchen with a vision she had in her mind. The thunder could still be heard in the distance, but it did not bother her anymore. Susan was more excited about the new activity she had found for herself. It gave her some comfort and a ray of hope to connect with her husband. She sat at the small country table and took off her cross necklace to get started with the readings. She placed it above the letters, but before she moved it, the cross started moving in different directions.

Susan was taken aback as she pulled her hand away from the cross; it was all too scary for her. She sat there still, watching the cross moving by itself.

"H"

"E"

"L"

"P"

Susan couldn't believe what she saw, and the cross was still moving.

"M"

"E"

Suddenly, her mind recalled the loud whisper she had heard in the dream last night.

"Help me!"

Susan once again found herself standing in the dark, as clueless as ever.

The cross didn't stop moving, and it spelled *"help me"* repeatedly.

She finally gathered the courage to ask the question. "Who are you?" she asked in a loud voice.

The cross didn't move. "What's your name?" Susan asked again when there was no movement.

"R"

There was sudden movement; it felt as if someone was forcefully dragging the cross. Susan watched closely as the cross moved from one alphabet to the other.

"O, S, E."

It was still moving.

"M, A, R, Y."

Susan sat there in disbelief as she read the name out aloud.

"Rosemary!"

She was trying to remember if it was someone she had known.

Heaps of questions jumbled up in her mind, and there was only one way to get the answers.

Chapter Two

Meeting Rosemary

Susan wasn't sure why she was feeling so needy and helpless. She had so much going on in her life than she could comprehend. Susan and her husband had a reputable law firm, but she had taken a leave to pull herself together. She needed some time to mourn the loss and heal from the trauma that was taking a toll on her mental health.

She crossed out and decided to contact Joe. Somewhere back in her mind, she already knew what to expect; she wasn't nervous this time.

"Joe, can you hear me?" she asked.

"Yes," Joe replied from the other side.

The two continued to talk; it had been so long since they caught up. Joe explained that he would see her again and assured her he was happy and safe.

"Promise me you will live your life to the fullest. Have fun, and don't work so hard."

Tears gleamed in her eyes as she uttered goodbye. Knowing that he was happy gave her a sense of satisfaction and closure.

She started thinking about James and wondered if she should tell him about the encounter with Rosemary. But she didn't; she didn't want anyone to worry about her as she was in the farmhouse alone.

The thunder had stopped, but it was not gone forever. Susan decided to have a cup of hot tea and thought about the events during the last few days. While lost in her thoughts, she received a call from James, who had an update about her order. Her sink and dishwater were all set to arrive, and James was going to help her install them. She was looking forward to their coffee plan the next morning.

Susan smiled once again as she went upstairs and got in bed. She had a productive day, and she was tired. But suddenly, she remembered something

— *Rosemary.*

She recalled her little experience from the night before, which introduced her to Rosemary. It had taken her some time to grasp what had happened and whether it was real. One thing she knew for sure was that the cross didn't move by itself, and there was some supernatural power involved in it.

Susan decided to try it again to see if it would happen again. She wondered if she could talk to Rosemary, then she would also be able to contact her husband; even the thought of it made her happy. She reached into her drawer and got her tarot cards and the fan. It was all like a movie again; the sound of strong wind against the window, the darkness outside, and the dim light bulb hanging on top of her. She gasped before she got started with all the courage she had.

"Rosemary, are you there?"

Susan saw no movement for the first few seconds. She almost lost hope before the cross moved all of a sudden.

"*Yes,*" a brief reply came.

Susan got a chill down her spine but continued with a straight face. She had already gotten a name and wanted to know more about her — Rosemary.

"What do you want, Rosemary?" Susan asked her purpose.

"*Answers,*" Rosemary replied.

"What happened to you?" Susan asked again.

The cross started moving; Susan kept her eyes glued to its movement as she read the words aloud, one after another.

"*I was murdered.*"

The hairs at the back of her neck and arms erected. However, Susan waited for Rosemary to continue.

"I was robbed and murdered. They buried me in the Mississippi River."

She felt anxious and scared with every word Rosemary made.

"I have been trying to reach the light ever since. I cannot see. I am buried deep down the dark water of the Mississippi River."

"Who did this to you?" Susan asked, concerned and worried at the same time. She didn't understand who could do such a thing to a person.

This time, Susan received no answer. The movement of the cross halted; Susan was startled by the abrupt roar of thunder. It was pouring down again, and the pattering of rain surrounded the silence.

Rosemary faded as if she was never there.

It took Susan a while to figure out the background story of Rosemary. She collected information in bits and pieces and tried to place them in order; it was like solving a riddle. As she was living alone in the farmhouse, Rosemary had sort of become her friend with whom she would talk till late at night, sometimes, till dawn.

The more and more Susan learned about Rosemary, the more she got attached to the girl — Rosemary felt like an old lost friend. The attachment grew when Susan forgot about her own distress — her heart started to feel the pain of what Rosemary had endured. This anguish took over her own distress.

It was a story she had never heard before.

***

In a small town in Mississippi, poverty knew no prejudice. Boys and girls worked in the field during the day, although the girls left early to help their moms with their chores. Rosemary's mother was a missionary, and she would always try to help others. She had built a cafeteria in an old warehouse called *The Mission House.*

The Mission House was the heartbeat of this small community. Everyone called Rosemary's mother *"V."* She would organize the mission with farmers and mothers to help feed many hungry people. She had two girls named Tanya, the oldest by three years, and Rosemary, the youngest. Although the girls were close in age, they were as different as night and day.

Tanya was a daydreamer and always looked for a way out of responsibility. She was not interested in studies or house chores but would spend hours looking through them. Her dream was to become a superstar in Hollywood, and that's what she would always think about.

On the other hand, Rosemary was always by her mother's side, helping her pack the meals and run errands. She would study hard at school and had a teacher who would give her lessons to learn at home. Her ultimate dream was to enroll in college with a scholarship.

Tanya and Rosemary were born in an old log cabin with giant trees in the background. Rosemary would often look out of the window and recall how she would play with her sister in the puddles when they were toddlers. Their father had died of a heart attack when they were toddlers, and their mother struggled to keep up with the farm.

V was left with no choice but to lease the land to other farmers for a small donation and a portion of the food for her mission house. As time passed, things got a little better. The schools opened up again, and the boys and girls could return on the first day of school.

Everyone was excited. The school had a big classroom for every two grades. Tanya was in the 11th grade because she was held back a year for poor attendance. On the other hand, Rosemary was promoted to the 10th grade because she studied all summer in her spare time and participated in extra- credit activities. Tanya and Rosemary shared the same classroom.

After school, Rosemary would rush back home; she remained loyal to her mother and knew she was now old enough to do everything on her own. Rosemary was now old enough to help with the bookkeeping and make deposits. She also helped prepare the food and still managed to keep up with her studies.

On the other hand, Tanya spent most of her time with her boyfriend, a high school senior. Rosemary also had a boyfriend, Ben, who was ambitious toward higher studies, just like her. Ben had his eyes set on the scholarship. Rosemary and her boyfriend worked hard in school and remained loyal to their roots, with big dreams for a better life.

On Wednesday service evenings, everyone would be energized by God's Grace and ask for forgiveness for their sins. A few young women and a married couple also joined the church. In the church, it was announced that the fall festival would be coming, and they should start preparing the venue and games.

Many people came from all other countries to experience this historic festival. There would be games for the children in different contests and prizes. Everyone joined hands and said Grace in the lunchroom, then ate together. The church kept this small community deeply connected.

The next day, they all made a list of all the activities and passed it down to Rosemary to delegate authority to the ones in charge. The day was long, and V went to bed. The two girls went to their room, which they shared. Tanya was exceptionally quiet.

"What's wrong?" Rosemary inquired.

Tanya was initially reluctant, but she admitted that she had a secret and that if she told her, she couldn't tell anyone, especially their mother.

Rosemary was skeptical about it because she didn't like keeping secrets from her mother. However, at that moment, she felt Tanya needed her.

"Okay, I promise," Rosemary assured her that she would not tell anyone.

Tanya then went on to share the secret that she had been keeping to herself. She told Rosemary that she was seeing an older man across the river. A few months ago, she had gone for dinner when Tanya came across this guy.

He was a good-looking older man who was there to eat dinner when he saw Tanya.

"Can I buy you dinner?" Tom had offered Tanya.

Tanya couldn't resist the offer when she found out that he was a famous movie producer in Hollywood. He lived in California and was in the town for a visit when he met Tanya. For Tanya, it was like her dream knocking at the door; she had always wanted to be a Hollywood star, and there was a walking-talking opportunity in front of her.

"We both love each other. I am thinking about running away with him to California." Tanya shared her enthusiasm.

It wasn't love; she knew that for sure.

Rosemary was speechless; her heart felt heavy and burdened. She now knew her secret and didn't know how to go about it. "Maybe you should talk to Mom about your plans so we can meet this Mr. Man who has stolen my sister's heart," she suggested in a friendly manner, trying her best not to agitate Tanya to take a drastic measure.

"What about John, your boyfriend?" Rosemary suddenly remembered.

Tanya was very casual when she said she only sees John for appearances.

"I will be eighteen in six months. I have a whole life ahead," she added.

Rosemary asked her sister to take a little time and think about her decision. But deep down in Tanya's heart, she knew she didn't have time.

The next day the girls went about their routine, school, chores, and preparing for the festival. As weeks went by, Tanya started getting sick. Her mom thought she had the flu and made her stay in bed. Tanya knew that it was not the flu; she was pregnant. She decided to use this time to meet her lover, who would be coming into town that day. She was planning to tell him that she was pregnant.

Darkness persisted as the days became shorter. The small town prepared to face the danger ahead of the thunderstorm.

During this time, Rosemary tried keeping her eyes on Tanya as much as possible because she didn't want her to run away with a guy named Tom, whom no one had met.

Late in the afternoon, the rain commenced to pour down. The thunder roared, and lightning flashed. The advisory warning said to stay indoors. Rosemary was worried because she couldn't find Tanya. Rosemary's mother entered the room and asked if she had seen Tanya.

"Not since I saw her with Sam cleaning all the tubs for Apple bobbing," Rosemary told her the truth.

Rosemary hoped she would go to Sam's house to eat dinner with them and would come home when the rain let up. The following day there was still no sign of Tanya. Rosemary left her mother a note saying she had to go to the general store for something and would return as early as possible. On the street, Rosemary noticed everyone working around the houses, cleaning up limbs and debris… and when she entered the general store, Ms. Miller had a letter sealed in an envelope addressed to Rosemary. With sweaty hands, Rosemary opened the envelope. She straightened the crumbled sheet inside to read the inked words:

"Dear sister, I had to leave with Tom because I'm carrying his baby. Yes, I'm pregnant. Tell Mom I love her and not to worry.

I'm in good hands with Tom. I will write you and Mom and let you know how I'm doing. Please don't cry; just know I am happy and love you both.

Love,

Tanya."

The sun was trying to break through the clouds and shine down on their small Mississippi town. When Rosemary returned home, she was speechless; Rosemary didn't hesitate to take the letter to her mother.

Rosemary was tired of running errands, so she walked outside. As she watered the roses, she felt uneasy, as if someone was watching her.

Far into the distance, she could see the winding trail leading to the Mississippi River. With her sister and friends, she would sneak away from home sometimes and hang out or go for a swim on hot summer days. Again, Rosemary could swear that she saw someone in the bushes across the road, but there was no one to be seen. She shrugged it off and went about her day.

The days seemed longer, and the nights appeared shorter — time was slipping away, weeks became months, and she still heard no word from Tanya. Rosemary's mother was quieter than usual and tried to stay busy since Tanya's departure. Months passed, and everyone started preparing for the fall festival; thus, no one paid attention.

The next day Rosemary went to Mississippi to help her mom prepare the lunchroom for dinner later that night. Upon Rosemary's arrival, she immediately handed the rosters and posters to have copies made. When she entered the post office, Ms. Miller greeted everyone with a smile.

"Good afternoon, Ms. Miller," Rosemary greeted her. "Mom has sent over to have copies made."

"It would take about an hour to complete all the rosters and posters for the festival, and you could also pick them up the next morning," she replied.

"I'll be back in an hour," Rosemary informed Ms. Miller when she saw Ben outside from the window. It had been a long since the two caught up on life. She went straight to him.

"Ben!" she almost yelled to catch his attention.

Ben turned toward her; his eyes lit up when he saw Rosemary approaching him. He grabbed her away and swirled her around, expressing how glad he was to see her. Rosemary blushed.

"Where has my true love been?" he joked lovingly.

Rosemary and Ben both got scholarships.

She told him she was helping her mom prepare for the fall festival.

"Where have you been?" she asked Ben this time.

"I have been helping my dad with the fall crops. Maybe I can get off early tomorrow to help with the festival," he replied.

"It would be great," Rosemary thought they both would have more time to spend together.

The meeting with Ben was brief. Rosemary returned to the post office and picked up the posters and rosters.

To her surprise, an envelope was there, addressed to her name; it was a letter from Tanya.

"Dear Rosemary,

I am writing to inform you that I'll be coming home to meet you and mom after the festival.

Take good care of mom and yourself. Love,

Tanya."

The next day, Ben was standing at the front door, smiling brightly. He had come to help distribute the posters and pass out rosters to all participants. Involved with the festival, Rosemary's Mother cooked a big breakfast and invited Ben to eat with them. After breakfast, they got to work immediately, and it felt like old times working with her best friend.

The day went by quickly as they finished up and returned to The Mission House, where her mother asked her to make a deposit. The deposit was a large sum with all the festival funds added. Ben was kind enough to escort her to the bank. On the way, the two kept conversing; Rosemary felt good and secure having Ben by her side.

As the two walked down the street, Rosemary again felt like someone was watching her. She felt a gaze boring into her.

"Do you see it?" she asked anxiously.

"What?" Ben seemed clueless.

"I think someone is following us or watching us," she shared her suspicion with Ben about what she had been feeling lately.

Ben assured her that there was no one and that it might just be her imagination. Rosemary didn't want to press the issue, but she had been feeling uneasy for the past few days. The festival was in the next week, and everyone was excited. However, Rosemary couldn't help but wonder what must have happened to Tommy, Tanya's best friend. The two had been best friends since the first grade.

Since Tanya had chosen a different life for her, and she was apparently happy in it too, but Rosemary's heart sank when she thought about Tommy and how lonely he must be feeling around this time of the year. She felt sorry for him.

At the same time, Rosemary was excitedly looking forward to the next day. She knew Ben would be there to help her with the festival, so she put in extra effort to look special.

Excitement was in the air, and the townspeople could feel it in their hearts. Suddenly, she heard a knock at the door. Ben was there early, and his eyes sparkled at Rosemary's gorgeous appearance, and he showered her with compliments.

"Good morning, beautiful," he hugged her before they left.

Rosemary couldn't stop smiling as they walked down the street to The Mission House. She had to pick up her mother's deposit; they picked up the deposits and continued into town. Rosemary had no clue that Ben had arranged a surprise for her; she kept walking as usual.

Ben walked closely by Rosemary's side with a gentle smug smile, the same smile he would have when he was up to something since the first grade.

Although he tried to keep the surprise a secret, his eyes couldn't hide his excitement. Rosemary knew he was up to something.

"What is it?" she asked as she noticed the gentle smug smile on his face. "Hhhmm. Nothing," he said, grinding his teeth.

As they walked down the street, Rosemary stopped by the post office to get the mail. She hoped there would be a new letter from her sister, but there was none. She was disappointed at first but admired her sister's confidence and ability to make friends quickly. Rosemary wanted Tanya to be safe and happy; she was also proud of her sister for achieving her dreams.

She returned to the street where Ben was waiting for her, and they both continued walking. All the while, Rosemary felt as if a little shadow had been tagging along everywhere she went. She was taken aback when Ben grabbed her out of nowhere.

"I'm taking you out!" he told her, smiling ear to ear.

He further told her that he parked his dad's truck just around the corner so he could surprise Rosemary.

"I've been saving for a long time so that we can eat at a nice restaurant. My dad told me about a restaurant in the next town," his tone was filled with enthusiasm.

Rosemary's heart swelled with all the love she had for him; she was surprised and excited as she had never eaten out before. She didn't want her mother to worry, so she decided to swing by the Mission to inform her. "Don't worry, mom. I'll be back soon," she told her mom.

"Have a good time," the mother replied with a smile.

Ben and Rosemary felt glad as Mother V approved, and now they could enjoy the evening to the fullest. The two kept driving for hours and were on the verge of giving up as they struggled to find a restaurant. They soon came to the bridge crossing the Mississippi; across the bridge, the traffic got heavier and hit the street. The streets were lit with beautiful white lights, and Rosemary couldn't take her eyes off them.

Finally, they saw the restaurant on the right, just like Ben's father described. He pulled into the car, and the two went inside the restaurant. The place was fancy and extremely beautiful. The two sat at a table by the window; the evening seemed magical. The waiter immediately came to their table to take their order.

"Would you like to share a seafood platter?" Rosemary asked Ben. She was being polite as she didn't want Ben to spend extravagantly.

However, Ben had everything planned. He told Rosemary that she should have her own platter while he would get the same for himself. Both of them also ordered iced tea.

Ben put his hand on Rosemary's hands and expressed his feelings.

"I love you. You are my best friend and the love of my life," he said with moist eyes.

Rosemary's cheeks turned crimson; she had always loved him, even when he pulled her pigtails in the first grade. She reminded him of that incident.

"Haha. Sure, you can hold onto a grudge," he laughed.

The waiter arrived with the iced tea and placed it in front of them. "The food is on the way," with this, he left. It didn't take long as a young man approached them again, but this time with two huge platters stacked up with more seafood than the two had imagined.

While enjoying the meal, Ben took out a box and smiled at Rosemary. He handed her the box, and Rosemary saw a beautiful gold necklace inside it.

"Oh, my God. It's beautiful!" she remarked as tears filled her eyes.

Rosemary put the cross around her neck, and Ben fastened it. She leaned her head on his shoulders; Ben felt good about Rosemary sitting close to him.

"It's getting late, and we must get back home," he said as he glanced outside the glass window; it was getting darker with each passing second.

"Yes. We must," Rosemary replied. It was an evening to remember; Rosemary had not felt this good in a long time. Suddenly, she forgot about the shadow following her at every step. But the longing to meet Tanya still lingered somewhere deep inside her heart.

Chapter Three

The Beginning

"Tanya, come here. Look what I found!" Little Rosemary cried at the top of her lungs. She was moving up and down on her feet, tightly holding something in her hands.

"What is it?" Tanya asked from a distance.

Rosemary was standing in a puddle on the bank of the Mississippi river; her feet were covered with mud, but it didn't bother her.

The chocolate brown soil had patches of virescent green; the dark heavy clouds hung over them, threatening a thunderstorm. A dreary light enveloped the world; these smoky capricious guests obstructed every sunray.

Tanya came hoping toward Rosemary as she tried to avoid the wet patches of mud to not dirty her pretty pink pumps.

"What is it?" she asked impatiently, leaning a little toward the tied hands.

Rosemary looked at her with sparkling eyes; a grin danced on her face. She was about 4-5 years old, while her sister was a few years older. She slowly opened her fist, and there lingered a beautiful red stone. They gave a light gleam even in the dull light bestowed by the cover of clouds.

"Isn't it beautiful?" she lisped, smiling ear to ear.

"It's just a stone. Huff, I thought you had found a diamond!" Tanya spat and threw the pebble into the river before returning to practice her dance moves again.

The pebble struck the water's surface with a plop; Rosemary stared at the ripples; fat tears commenced tumbling her chubby cheeks. For little Rosemary, that beautiful pebble she found in the dirt was more precious than any jewel.

The rustic hues of the submerged pebbles in the river had awakened Rosemary's memories as she passed by the Mississippi River ahead of the festival. She watched the ducklings float on the surface like broken leaves on water; it was a salve to her mind, and she wondered how many mysteries were stored in the dept of the vast stagnant river.

The sight of the Mississippi River reminded her of how far she had come. As a little girl, she would often visit the riverside with her sister Tanya who was now miles away from her, living her own life.

She recalled the time when she would play with her sister all day long and did not have a care in the world. Rosemary didn't have many friends, and she looked up to Tanya whenever she felt lost. However, as they grew up, the sisters grew distant. While Rosemary would spend most of her time studying and helping her mother out, Tanya had her circle of friends with whom she spent most of her time.

Things were not so bad until Rosemary discovered that Tanya had become addicted to drugs. One fine morning, the two sisters were alone in the house while their mother had gone to church. Rosemary woke up to a disturbance when she saw Tanya moving restlessly around the room.

"What happened?" Rosemary inquired with a frown.

"Have you seen my bag?" Tanya asked as if she was running out of time; her eyes were watery, and her hands were quivering.

"No. But what happened?" Rosemary asked again, wide awake. The frown turned deeper.

Before she could utter another word, Tanya exclaimed, "Oh, there it is!" She had to struggle to drag out her bag from under the bed.

Rosemary watched her shockingly as Tanya grabbed a small bag filled with white powder and snorted it. Rosemary sat there numb, watching her sister act like the drug addicts she would see under the bridge on her way back from church. The same people her mother would tell her to stay away from.

"If you tell mother, you are dead!" Tanya threatened her in her own older sister manner. "It's just a one-time thing, no big deal," she added, hoping Rosemary would let it go.

Rosemary did not want Tanya to feel more distant from her or their mother; thus, she decided to keep her mouth shut. She trusted Tanya when she assured her that she would never do it again. At the same time, Rosemary had uncovered the reason behind Tanya's disconnected nature and mood swings, and she wanted to help her out of it. However, it was yet another secret between the two sisters that no one else knew.

After many years, these memories resurfaced as Rosemary missed Tanya more than ever. Seeing Tanya's face again had become a longing, which rested heavily on Rosemary's chest. With the festival around the corner, she was helping her mother in the church, but everything about her life reminded her of her older sister.

As Rosemary walked down the street, she felt like someone was watching her again. She turned around, but there was no one, but she could still feel the uncanny presence. She began to stride, increasing the pace of her feet to a run. When she heard muffled footsteps approaching her, she turned anxious; she turned back again; sweat beads slipped down her face.

"Rosemary!" a guy called her name and stood just a few feet away.

"John!"

It was a sigh of relief; Rosemary calmed down to see a familiar face.

"What is it?" she asked.

"I'm sorry. I didn't mean to scare you. I thought … I-I thought…" John broke into tears before he could even finish his sentence, "I thought Tanya was here. I've heard rumors about her, and I'm worried."

Rosemary recalled how close Tanya was to her best friend, John. However, when she left town, Tanya did not even bother to inform John. Rosemary knew that if there was someone who knew Tanya better than her, it was John.

"Tanya will be visiting after the festival," Rosemary said softly.

"I'm anxious to see her. I think something is wrong," John let out worriedly. "Can you meet me tomorrow?" he requested Rosemary.

After a short while, Rosemary answered with a nod.

Soon enough, John told her that he was busy helping his father with the crops and the butchering, so he could not stay longer. However, he did mention that he knew something about Tanya that Rosemary must know.

Rosemary trusted John and knew he truly cared about Tanya. She decided to meet John the next day, hoping he would help her figure out Tanya's whereabouts.

***

It had become a routine for Susan to talk to Rosemary and learn more about her story. Susan would finish all her chores and look forward to going upstairs to talk to her new friend, whom she only knew. Since Rosemary had to spell every word out for Susan, it took months for her to know her, her origin, her family, and all the other things.

Meanwhile, as she was trying to know her way around the farmhouse, she had also become good friends with James. He would be there for her whenever she needed him, even if it was for the slightest inconvenience. Their friendship ticked off ever since James had helped Susan install the kitchen sinks and the dishwasher. As promised, he was standing at her front door at 8:00 am; the two had a good chat over the morning coffee before they started work.

The two bonded very well from the beginning and enjoyed spending time together. It was a much-needed change for Susan to pull her up from the turmoil she had experienced not long ago.

While James had proven to be a good friend, Susan was still unsure if she should tell him about Rosemary. What if he thinks

I'm crazy? Or making up stories in my head? This fear stopped her from sharing anything with James. At the same time, Rosemary still needed to complete her story, as Susan still did not know who her murderer was.

Susan had invited James to lunch the next day; she had decided to talk to him about it as he was familiar with this place. James was the only one she knew in the new neighborhood, and Susan had no other shoulder to rely on. While there were still many aspects of the story to be unveiled, Susan knew the location of the house where Rosemary lived, and it was not far away.

The next day, Susan got ready and prepared a delicious lunch as James was going to come over. The lunch comprised buttered chicken roast, mashed potatoes, and herbed rice. The aroma of the food filled the air in the house.

As always, James arrived at the promised time. Susan felt excited to see him. In the wild neighborhood, the warmth of his presence made Susan feel comfortable and at peace.

"Oh, something smells great!" James inhaled the aroma. "What have you cooked?" he asked, grinning as he entered the living room.

It made Susan feel special.

"Mashed potatoes and roasted chicken with rice," Susan replied as she served him.

Over lunch, the two talked about their personal lives and how living in a farmhouse was different than living in the city. As they were halfway through eating lunch, Susan opened her mouth again.

"James, I want to tell you something," she said.

"What is it?" James asked with concern.

"Whatever I'm going to tell you, you must believe it's not something I have made up in my mind," Susan was cautious before she even began.

"You can trust me, Susan. Now, tell me what it is?" James asked again politely.

Susan gasped before she started telling him about Rosemary. She had to tell the story from the beginning, back to the night when she first interacted with Rosemary. She told James about Rosemary's mother and Tanya and how they lived in a small house near the Mississippi River.

"She was murdered, and her body was thrown in the river," Susan finished her sentence.

She looked at James, who had not spoken a word; he just stared at her, astonished. Susan had shared every detail she knew about Rosemary, hoping that James wouldn't judge her or break her trust.

"What else do you know about this girl?" James asked with scrunched brows.

"I have her address. If that helps?"

Susan showed him the address she had written down on a piece of paper.

"Let's go and find out more," James said, determined.

Susan felt relieved that James trusted her and that he was already willing to help her figure out what had happened to Rosemary.

The place was not very far, and Susan and James decided to walk. It was a pleasant afternoon, and the two shared laughs along the way, enjoying each other's company while walking along the still water of the Mississippi River, which only danced with the strong gush of the wind.

"Look, there is an old Oak tree." James pointed toward a property; there was a giant tree, but the land was flooded.

Susan took a deep breath before she walked toward it. The place was exactly how Rosemary had described it, and for a moment, Susan couldn't believe her eyes.

Am I dreaming? Or is this actually Rosemary's house?

The same Rosemary who she had not even met, the mysterious girl who was murdered and whose body was left to be drowned in the depths of the river — the girl's house rested before her; as if waiting for her to enter.

Susan squeezed James's hands and looked him in the eyes; together, they were ready to embark on this quest to find out who killed *Rosemary.*

Chapter Four

Run Away

The thunder was loud, and the rain was pouring down as Rosemary aired it out the window. Her heart was still longing to see her sister and to meet again. It seemed like years since Rosemary heard from Tanya, but it did not stop her from worrying about her every day.

The historical fall festival finally concluded with immense success. Ms. V had done a remarkable job uplifting the community and raising funds for the unprivileged. Moreover, hundreds of people visited her café, and it was crowded throughout the festival. Almost the whole village participated; the festival evoked a sense of belonging in the community and brought people together.

The event was a breath of freshness amidst the gloominess surrounding the town following the recession. It also gave Rosemary and Ms. V something to focus on other than worrying about Tanya and her whereabouts.

There were newspapers from the larger towns doing a story on Ms. V and the community. The reporters visited the town, took many pictures of Ms. V, and interviewed her. Later, they published an account of the community's survival and services during and after the depression.

Since Tanya had promised to visit them after the festival, Rosemary anxiously awaited her arrival. She was very discontent and worried about Tanya; she felt she needed to do something, so she grabbed the raincoat and umbrella and told her mom that she would check the mail. Ms. V had tried to stop her, but Rosemary was determined to go out, and she told her mother she had to do something important.

It was a bit chilly outside; Rosemary looked around as she shoved her hands in her raincoat pockets. As Rosemary started walking toward her destination, she heard a soft voice call her name.

"Rosemary."

She quickly turned back to see who it was, but there was no one. It was a familiar neighborhood; the same old damp sand, giant trees, and the untamed Mississippi River flowed ruthlessly along the town. The moment she started walking again, someone called her again; this time, it was a clear, loud voice.

"Rosemary!"

It was coming from behind the clustered bunch of oak trees; Rosemary saw the leaves moving as if someone was hiding there.

"Who is there?" she asked, trying to gather every ounce of strength and courage to take a step further. "Rosemary, here. It's me," the voice grew louder with each step, and what Rosemary saw next left her in shock.

"It's me, Tanya!"

It was Tanya hiding behind the trees; she put her fingers over her mouth, moderating and motioning for Rosemary to be quiet.

Rosemary quickly walked toward her sister. "What's with all the secrecy?" she whispered.

She was seeing Tanya after a long time and had many questions to ask.

Tanya told her to be quiet and that they needed to talk openly elsewhere.

"Let's walk over to John's house, and I'll explain everything," Tanya said as she started walking.

Rosemary followed her.

"John? How does John know about Tanya?" Rosemary wondered as she recalled bumping into John the other day, who said he

had something to tell her. *"Did John already know that Tanya was in town? Was he hiding it from everyone else?* But *why would he do that?"*

So many questions flocked inside her mind as Rosemary walked with Tanya toward John's house. She already knew that John was Tanya's ex- boyfriend, but the last she knew was that Tanya got married to Tom and moved to California. *"When did she move back here? And that, too, in John's house?"* "What about the baby?" Rosemary couldn't stop herself from asking where the baby was.

"The baby is at John's. He is his father; I lied about the timing. I'll explain more when we reach John's."

When they reached John's house, it was all too shocking for Rosemary to grasp. John was talking to a small infant boy in a rocking chair, and Rosemary's eyes filled with tears. He was the cutest child she had ever seen and was so perfect.

"What is his name?" Rosemary asked.

She was his aunt, and her heart swelled with love as she held his small hands and gently kissed his tiny feet.

"John. I named him John the III," Tanya told Rosemary, who looked at her with questioning eyes. Tanya knew that it was the moment that she needed to explain everything in detail.

"When I realized that Tom was doing drugs and had abusive behavior, I started planning the escape," Tanya explained as she watched John rocking the baby.

His eyes sparkled; John wanted Tanya and the baby to stay with him so he could protect them.

"But protect them from whom?"

Rosemary could not have been happier to see Tanya back, and seeing the baby was a cherry on top. She was excited and wanted to take them home to see Mother V, but Tanya made an excuse.

"I want to go home also, but I'm too scared and ashamed," Tanya spoke the truth.

Rosemary understood her situation and told her that she would let her mother know her story, so she came over with John.

"I will go ahead now and return off and tell mom your story. You can come over with John and the baby later today when no one can see you in the dark," Rosemary told Tanya before departing.

The day had turned out to be very exciting so far. Rosemary ran home with excitement in her heart; she had not felt so happy in a while. She couldn't wait to reach home so she could share this news with her mother.

"Rosemary, is this you?" Ms. V yelled as she heard her enter the house.

Rosemary immediately ran into the room as she did not want her mother to worry about her safety.

"What's wrong? Are you okay?" Ms. V asked as she saw Rosemary enter the room.

"Yes, mother. Everything is fine. You need to calm down," Rosemary tried to calm her down and poured her a glass of water. She then sat by her bedside so she could tell her about Tanya. The happiness in her eyes was evident; Ms. V wondered what it was that she needed to tell her.

"Tanya is back. She is in town and has a baby," she finally revealed with sparkling eyes.

"Where?" Ms. V asked as her eyes filled with tears.

Rosemary calmly explained to her what had happened earlier that day. "Mom, it turns out that Tanya's boyfriend uses drugs and has threatened the baby and her life. Tanya is so sorry for running away. She thought life would have been better for the baby and herself, but she didn't realize that she had a good life at home, around people she loved."

Rosemary also told her mother that Tanya was pregnant with John's child before she left with Tom, "She has a little boy, and he looks just like John. They must be on their way over because it's almost dark."

Ms. V was excited to meet Tanya after a long time. She prepared some drinks and sandwiches to welcome John and Tanya as they were coming home together for the first time. Moreover, she was happily looking forward to finally meeting her grandchild.

When it was around 7 o'clock in the evening, Tanya arrived at the residence; she entered from the back door and went straight to hug her mother. Ms. V could not hold back the tears of joy and immediately took the baby in her arms. That was the moment Ms. V felt perfectly content after a long time.

"I have prepared sandwiches for you. Please go on and have a bite or two, and don't worry about the baby; he's in good hands," Ms. V told the three of them while rocking little John in her arms.

Rosemary, Tanya, and John circled around the table. They started talking about the festival and how well it went and helped so many people. John also reminisced about how his dad could pay his seed bills and taxes after giving Ms. V her share of the mission and had little money left for any emergency.

After so many days, giggles echoed inside the small house that was haunted by loneliness and wilderness that prevailed alongside the Mississippi River. The evening turned brighter when John called everyone around the table and proposed to Tanya.

"Will you marry me?" he asked as he looked at her with all the love he had for her.

John had already planned the entire thing. He promised Tanya that they would continue school at night and grow together in every step of life. His dad had already allowed the two of them to live with him with the child.

"I would love to be your wife. But… it's just too dangerous, and what if you change your mind when you hear my story?" Tanya raised suspicions. After what had happened with Tom, she worried about her child's safety.

"I know you better than you know yourself. I love you because you are a daydreamer and always want to do better. I never want to hold you back from opportunity, and I want to hold your hand and keep you safe and loved," John assured her.

John's proposal offered a much-needed relief in Tanya's already chaotic life; she could not resist the proposal and said, *"Yes!"*

"Congratulations," Ms. V smiled as she came to hug Tanya. She asked her to stay with her for the night so she could spend more time with her and the baby. Rosemary also asked her to stay, and Tanya eventually agreed.

Growing up, Rosemary had seen Tanya spend most of her time with John, who always seemed to be so much in love with her. She was happy that her sister finally made the right decision, especially after she made the mistake of running away with the older guy. She looked at John and Tanya as they sat there with each other, holding hands. It was like a fairytale come true — but who knew what was coming next?

After dinner, John left with the assurance that he would check on them and look out for any stranger in the community. Tanya and Rosemary had a lot to catch up on, and as they chatted, they also built a safety plan. Tanya was nervous that Tom would be looking for her.

"I couldn't understand why you left us," Rosemary expressed how confused she was about Tanya's decisions for herself and the baby.

Tanya agreed that she had made a mistake.

"When I realized that Tom had anger issues, I started planning to get out of that place. I think Tom knew something was up, but that did not stop him from going out for days drinking and partying. This time when he left, I packed baby's stuff and mine and headed straight to catch the bus," Tanya shared the details of the day when she escaped from the house.

Although it sounded very dangerous, Rosemary was grateful that she was now safe and with her family. Throughout the time, Ms. V couldn't take her eyes off her grandson; he was so beautiful and perfect.

"Relax. Maybe he had moved on with his miserable addiction," Rosemary assured Tanya as the two observed Ms. V playing with the baby; she was so excited that day that she even started planning Tanya's and John's wedding.

The festival had concluded with great success, and now they had a wedding to plan. Everyone was talking about how the festival was and how well it went. Ms. V was now looking forward to arranging Tanya's wedding at the mission. She could not wait to hold her grandson at the altar as her oldest daughter would marry the love of her life.

Chapter Five

Death

"Are you sure about this?" James looked at Susan, who wanted to visit Rosemary's house as if it was calling out to her.

"Uh-Uhm. I guess. Let's do this," Susan hesitated at first but then showed determination to get done with it.

They planned to explore the old house to look for clues that would lead them to Rosemary's death. On this little quest, Susan had packed a picnic lunch and some drinks to carry along. Given the circumstances, the drinks surely came in handy as Susan felt thirsty due to her growing anxiety and restlessness. James had arrived in his truck on time to pick Susan up; the two then drove to the abandoned house.

They were now standing in silence in front of Rosemary's house. It was a wooden house with a small door in the middle and two rustic windows on each side. The small dirt front yard was covered with uneven grass and wild shrubs growing; it looked like no one had trimmed the field in many years.

Throughout the ride, Susan's mind was locked in her conversations with Rosemary during the past few weeks. When she arrived at the property, Susan felt a connection with the place; she couldn't figure out why but she instantly felt familiar with the place she was visiting for the first time.

Susan stood still as her eyes gazed at the property. She looked up and down and couldn't help but ask herself, "Have I been here before?"

In normal circumstances, anyone walking the property would think they had stumbled on an old historic site and found it amusing enough to explore. However, Susan knew nothing was normal; something was hidden behind this backdrop of darkness and silence. She looked at James, who was slowly walking around the property with his hands in the side pockets of his jacket. It looked like he was following the footsteps of some animal crawling on a damp mud road.

Susan decided to go inside the house and see what she could find there. Now that she had spent a few minutes in silence, her anxiety had decreased, and she was ready to take matters into her hands. As Susan walked through the old wooden door, a high-pitched scream startled her. She didn't know what it was, but she went straight into James' arms, who was standing at a distance. Susan's heart was beating faster than ever; James's calmed her down.

"It's just a cat. Look!" James chuckled as he pointed his finger toward the black cat running into the bushes. It disappeared into the darkness the very next moment. This little incident got Susan scared. James slid her off his body and lightly patted her head. He then laughed and said calmly, "I better go first!"

This time, James slowly opened the door and entered the house; Susan followed him. Dim light was coming through the glass windows that had turned opaque due to all the dirt; Susan saw old wooden furniture covered in dust. After they entered the house, they realized it was not so bad. There was a small wooden table in the center of what looked like the living room and a wooden cupboard in one corner. James and Susan decided to pack everything that would help them get closer to Rosemary's killer. They packed the books, papers, and anything that looked worthy of investigation and put them in the trunk.

"Did you get the feeling that someone was watching us?" Susan asked James as they were about to leave.

James lifted his head and looked around the woods, then shuffled and got in the car. There would be moments when Susan could not guess what to expect from James, but deep down in her heart, she found him quite charming. Amidst all the gloominess, darkness, and mystery, he was the one who made her laugh.

Since Susan arrived at the farmhouse, James had been her only friend. Today, he even accompanied her to Rosemary's house without judging or making her feel insecure. James saw that Susan was stressed and stayed with her to figure out their next step.

Now, the two were sitting in her father's office; in front of them, there was a box of old books, newspapers, and other stuff that once, perhaps, belonged to Rosemary. As they started going through the stuff, they got their hands on new findings and clues to link the information together.

It was like Susan was holding a tangled wool yarn; she was unraveling the mystery behind Rosemary's death by piecing the puzzle together bit by bit.

***

As her family was now preparing for the wedding of Tanya and John, Rosemary was glad to see them all happy and united after a long time. As time passed, Tanya and Little John had also gotten comfortable with their surroundings. Little John was now growing and trying to walk; he was the light of their lives. Meanwhile, John was doing well on the farm, helping his father with the crops. This reunion had also given them an opportunity for Tanya and Rosemary to rekindle their bond; the two sisters now appeared closer than ever before.

At the same time, Rosemary was helping Ms. V at The Mission House. She would help her mother run errands in the kitchen and make deposits in the bank. It was one usual day when Rosemary woke up and was not feeling well. Still, she went to The Mission House at the church, where she found her mother working in the kitchen.

"Good morning, mother. Can I help you today?" Rosemary asked Ms. V.

"Of course, you can. I always appreciate your help, and I don't think I could do what I do without you," Mother V replied with a smile. It was her way of appreciating Rosemary's assistance.

Rosemary just nodded with a smile and started working. Later, she got the deposits together and told Ms. V she was going to the bank. As Rosemary was walking down the street, she came across many familiar faces who knew her as Ms. V's daughter. A few of them came to Rosemary and asked about Tanya and if she had returned from California. It got Rosemary confused; Tanya had been home for so long, but no one even saw her at the festival. She wondered how Tanya was roaming around so freely; she didn't look scared about Tom finding her whereabouts anymore.

"Is she secretly meeting Tom again?" Rosemary couldn't help but wonder, given how Tanya had behaved in the past. The fact that everything was going so smoothly got her suspicious, and her mind started speculating all the possible reasons. Rosemary made the deposits and checked the mail but never bothered to check behind her. After Rosemary left the post office, she glanced toward the path leading to the Mississippi River, where she would often come to visit with Tanya. Her keen sense of direction seemed to fade; the tall bush appeared to be moving in front of her continued. There was no movement until she completely exhausted herself.

"Hello, is anyone there?" she asked loudly.

There was no answer; her voice echoed back into her ears. She sprang back in what she thought was the direction of the town. However, the path ended at a slew in the river with high rocks right above the surface of the river water. Rosemary slowly moved toward the bushes, following the noise when she heard Tanya and Tom arguing about money.

"Unbelievable!" she thought she was scared and sat quietly behind the bush, near the rocks.

The arguing had dissipated; Rosemary wanted to get home so she could comfort Tanya. It was getting late as the darkness grew around her with each passing second. Rosemary was frozen in time and couldn't move; she wasn't sure what was happening or what to make up for it. She didn't even have the strength to get up and walk to the land. The sound of thrusting river water echoed amidst the silence in the woods. As far as she could see, there was a swarm of giant trees and dark river water flowing ruthlessly.

"Mother!" Rosemary knew her mother would be looking for her. She wanted to return home as soon as possible and decided to regain her bearings where she was.

***

When Tanya returned home, she went straight to The Mission House to see her mother, V.

"Have you seen Rosemary? She should have been home hours ago," Mother V asked the moment she saw Tanya entering the kitchen.

"Most likely, she stopped to see her nephew," Tanya replied. "I will help you in the kitchen," she then added and started working beside Mother V.

"That will be nice. You can update me on your wedding plans. We only have a week left," Mother V smiled as she looked at Tanya, who was carefully chopping down the vegetables.

Tanya didn't say anything and just smiled back. Mother V and Tanya worked and prepared dinner for the service they were holding later that night. Time flew by, and they managed to complete all the work in time. When it was late evening, they realized that Rosemary still hadn't returned home.

"I'm worried about Rosemary. She never goes out for hours without informing me," Mother V said as she walked back and forth. Her eyes were fixed on the glass window with concern in her eyes.

"I am worried about her, too. I'm leaving right now to see if she lost track of time." Tanya spoke up when she saw Mother V getting anxious.

"Thank you, Tanya." Mother V appreciated Tanya as she held Little John in her arms.

"But there has been no signs of Rosemary. Where are you going to find her? What if something happens to you, too?" This time it was John who worried about Tanya's safety.

Tanya assured him that she would take care of herself and asked him to stay close to the baby and not let anyone in. John wanted to go with her, but Tanya was more frightened about her little boy and wanted John to stay with the baby.

"It's okay. No matter what's going on or whatever happens, I'll always be there to protect our son. Be careful, and I love you!" John came near her and kissed her on the cheeks before Tanya left.

When Tanya arrived at the church, the service had already started. Tanya interrupted the service to tell everyone that Rosemary was missing. This news wreaked havoc at The Mission House as everyone got worried about Mother V's daughter going missing. Every man and woman who was able to search for her left the service. They all agreed to meet at the post office, and as soon as they got their lanterns, they formed groups. Men who knew the territory well led the teams. It was getting dark and still; they couldn't find a trace of Rosemary's whereabouts.

There were some women who stayed behind and formed a prayer room where they gathered to pray for Rosemary's safe return.

Thud. Thud.

There was a knock on the door, and it was Ben, Rosemary's boyfriend.

"I need to talk to you," Ben came straight to Tanya. He was almost in tears and wanted to talk to her. Tanya saw the distress on his face and asked him to follow her to the parlor, where the two sat to have a conversation.

"Where is Rosemary?"

Tanya's face turned red because she had told no one about Tom and the fact that she had been seeing him behind everyone's back. She explained to Ben that Tom had been following her and threatening her and her family, including her baby. She speculated that Tom had something to do with Rosemary's disappearance.

Ben was startled by what Tanya told him. His imagination was running vivid, and his mind was puzzled to make sense of everything. He loved Rosemary with all his heart and missed her dearly. After Mother V, he was probably the only person to miss Rosemary the most. Ben didn't say anything else to Tanya; he just got up and left.

"I'm sorry," Tanya yelled as she saw Ben walking out of the door. "I should have told someone!" The regret in her voice was evident.

Weeks turned into months, but Rosemary was nowhere to be found. However, none of them ever got tired and continued to look for her. It was a small town, and everyone who knew Rosemary loved her and was worried about her safety. Mother V felt as if she had lost a piece of her heart; after Rosemary's disappearance, her life was never the same.

Now, it had been years since they last saw Rosemary. Tanya and John got married, and their baby had now grown up to be a smart boy. On the other hand, Ben never stopped loving Rosemary and could never get over the loss. He had lost the love of his life, but he did continue to pursue higher studies, just as he and Rosemary had dreamed of together. He graduated college with honors and started teaching. However, he never got married.

Perhaps, he was still waiting for Rosemary to return.

***

"What do you think?"

Susan looked at James after they came across an old article entry where Tanya had arrived at the festival. It had been hours since Susan and James were going through the clues and old papers to figure *out who killed Rosemary.*

The more they studied the clues, the more suspicion fell on Tanya because she was the only one telling lies since the beginning. She didn't even tell anyone about meeting Tom; that was perhaps the reason why Rosemary's life was in danger in the first place.

Susan asked James if he would be okay to contact the clairvoyant. She wasn't sure if James was willing to delve further into this box of mysteries.

"Why not? We have come this far, and it wouldn't hurt to get to the bottom of it, right?" James nodded in approval. Susan smiled as she didn't have to do anything to convince James.

Susan got on to the computer right away and tried to contact the clairvoyant from whom she had bought the tarot cards. She tried multiple times and ended up leaving a message, hoping she would get back to her.

It was getting late, and James asked to leave. "I have to wake up early tomorrow. I'll see you tomorrow afternoon," he assured Susan before returning home. The following day, Susan was feeling good and decided to walk to Rosemary's house alone, where James was supposed to meet her. When she arrived, she noticed a dark cloud hovering close to the house's roof, which she thought looked unnatural.

"That's weird," she remarked as she once again looked around the property, but everything looked the same, other than the cloud. As she got closer, the cloud opened up, but there was no water. Susan started having second thoughts about going there alone; her heart started beating rapidly, and she wanted to go home.

Susan began to walk away when she heard a loud beating of a heart. She recalled that The Mission House was the heartbeat of the town. On her journey back to the house, she decided to wait on James before she could gather the courage to figure out the meaning behind the cloud.

Her heart was beating faster, and she didn't know how to make up for the darkness and the cloud that opened right in front of her eyes. Susan knew that there was something more to this story that was hidden somewhere beneath that very land.

She was determined to dig deeper into the pit of secrets until she got all the answers.

Chapter Six

Tracking Down

The sequel continued trying to follow Ghost n' Goblins. When Susan started this project, she thought she would write a simple story of truth as Rosemary had told her. She believed that it would set her spirit free, but she didn't think so anymore. Now that she had come all this way, she wondered if Rosemary had other plans for her. The more Susan tried to solve the mystery, the more she found herself entangled in it. What was supposed to be a peaceful getaway from the chaotic city life had turned into a thrilling adventure for her.

With each passing day, Susan felt more and more connected with Rosemary. She believed that Rosemary brought her to this house for a purpose, and she decided not to stop until she figured it out. Susan felt such a strong connection with Rosemary that it drove her to help her in every possible way. She kept wondering what she could do to help Rosemary reach the light. She also realized that she didn't even feel this connection with James.

While deep in her thoughts, Susan was startled to see James appear at the door. It was a pleasant surprise.

"Will you go to a ballroom dance with me tonight?" he asked her out of nowhere, fidgeting with the flowers he was holding. He was standing on the porch, looking nervous, as if he was asking her to a high school dance.

"Yes. Wow," Susan took flowers from his hands; the petals felt delicate on her fingertips. They were beautiful and smelled heavenly. "This is unexpected!" she added. Susan had no idea James wanted to take her to a dance amidst their little quest that was going side by side. Granted, she was looking forward to visiting Rosemary's house again with James, but a dance?

"Are you sure you want to take a break when we are so close to cracking this case, Sherlock?" she asked James playfully. Although she tried to make a point, she didn't want to refuse him directly. Moreover, how could she say no to dancing with James?

"Well, I kind of have to go. As I'm the President of the Cattleman's Association state-wide, they'll be expecting me there. If I don't go, it'll be rude," James told Susan why it was important for him to go to this dance. That was the first time James had shared anything about himself.

As soon as James revealed a little about himself, Susan's mouth dropped. She realized she didn't know much about James' life and who he was. Her arrogance was an embarrassment to herself, and she was almost speechless as she stood there staring right at him in total awe. While Susan was still figuring out what to say, James started laughing.

"What?" Susan asked shockingly.

"This is the first time I am seeing you at a loss for words. You look adorable!" James remarked, and Susan couldn't help but smile too.

Susan appreciated how James had been helping her with the case. Since the day she arrived at the farmhouse, he was there to help her. Be it setting up the kitchen sink or exploring an abandoned house in the woods, he was there with her. Now, she felt honored that he was asking her out on what appeared to be a special occasion.

"But I don't have anything to wear to the dance," Susan told James.

"Well, it's a semi-formal black-tie affair. C'mon, get in the truck. We'll figure something out," James asked her to follow him as he started walking outside.

Susan followed him to the door without a clue where he was going to take her. She got into the truck, and James started driving. They drove around mini curves over a bridge and pulled over in front of a cute little boutique.

"Maybe you can find something in there. I'll be right back!" James told Susan, pointing toward the store. Susan thought he must have some urgent stuff to deal with, given that he was a busy man. She stood there and watched him reverse the truck. She was now standing in front of the store.

"Let's do this, Susan," she gave herself a little pep talk as she couldn't recall the last time she went shopping alone.

Susan went inside the shop. She was amazed at the large collection of dresses as she browsed the racks. While scanning the store, Susan's eyes fell on a long, elegant, side-slit dress gown; it was strapless on one side. She fell in love with it after trying it on. It was intricately designed and looked stunning on display. When Susan tried it on, she couldn't help but fall in love with it.

The dress felt right out of a fairy tale. She kept staring at her reflection in the mirror for five minutes straight, turning back and forth; she loved how it fit perfectly, making her look more elegant and appealing. She decided to wear the gown to the dance, but as soon as Susan sought the price, she almost passed out. She was not entirely happy about it, but the gown fit her so well that she didn't want to miss the opportunity to wear it. She asked the saleswoman to pack it for her.

She also picked up a pair of cute pumps and a clutch bag to go with her dress. The saleswoman was friendly and nice. The moment she finished packing her stuff, James came in.

"You put that on my tab, Mary, didn't you?" he asked the receptionist.

"Yes. I did. Just as you asked," Mary told James.

"No, that's okay. I got this. Thank you," Susan told James that she would pay herself. However, James insisted, and ultimately, Susan had to agree.

"Thank you," Susan replied as she blushed.

They rushed home, and James told Susan he would come to pick her up in an hour. As James was about to walk out of the door,

Susan hugged him. The evening had proven to be lively so far, and Susan couldn't wait to see what was coming next. She then went inside to get ready for the dance.

Susan was excited because she had not been to a formal dance in years. As she was rushing to get dressed, she looked in the giant wall mirror. To her horror, she saw a face pressed against the glass window in the mirror reflection. For instance, she thought it was her imagination, but it was not. She turned back, but the face was still there, watching her closely. It was too blurry for her to figure out who it was, and Susan panicked. She was about to call James, but at the same moment, he showed up at her front door. *"How coincidental!"* she thought. But she was relieved that, at least, he was there.

"What's wrong?" James asked worriedly as he saw Susan shaking with fright when he entered the door. Her hands were trembling.

"Hey, what happened?" he asked with compassion.

"There… there was a face… pressed up… against my windo…" Susan was so scared that she found it difficult to even finish her sentence. "It was watching me," she added quietly after catching her breath.

James held her and comforted her. It took her a few minutes to relax in James' embrace, but she calmed down eventually. James turned back and wore his black hood and Toby boots; he went outside the main door to look at the window, but there was no one to be found.

"He must have left," James told Susan as he went inside again. This time, his big blue eyes lit up when he looked at her from head to toe.

"You. Look. Stunning," James remarked.

"Thank you," his compliment brought a smile to Susan's face.

"Close your eyes," James asked her as he took out a box from his pocket.

Susan closed her eyes, wondering what it might be.

"Now, look," he then asked Susan to look in the mirror. As Susan opened her eyes, she couldn't blink for a few seconds. Around her neck was the most beautiful diamond necklace she had ever seen. "It's beautiful. Thank you," she exulted.

"My pleasure," James smiled.

James made Susan feel very special with his gift. It had been a while since Susan felt actually alive. All the thoughts of the face in the window escaped her mind; she was now looking forward to spending the rest of the evening with James.

***

When they arrived at the ballroom, all the eyes were on Susan. As the President of the Cattleman's Association, James had to go up on stage and give a speech. Susan found him impressive, especially with his dry humor jokes.

The music started playing a slow song, and James pulled Susan onto the dance floor. As their feet were moving to the melodious tune, James pulled her close and whispered in her ears, "Thank you for coming."

Susan leaned back and smiled, "Oh, my pleasure."

Susan and James enjoyed the dance; they left the ballroom with many pleasant memories of the evening to be cherished for a long time. James drove her back to the house, and throughout the ride, they kept talking. Upon their arrival at the house, as James was pulling into the drive, Susan spotted a child who was hiding behind the big oak tree.

"Do you see him? James, look!" Susan yelled, pointing her finger toward the oak tree.

James just looked at her and asked, "See who?"

Susan paused for a moment. She wasn't sure if she should tell James because it could all be her imagination. She decided to keep it to herself and then calmly replied, "It was nothing. Just a dog."

The two went inside the house, had a cup of coffee, and expressed how enjoyable their evening was. Just when Susan thought James was about to leave, he stood up and announced that he was spending the night. "I would sleep on the daybed right outside your room."

Susan thought it was bold of him to make such an announcement without asking. But at the same time, she thought it was sexy, and it gave her a feeling of comfort, especially after the incidents she had experienced earlier that evening.

As James began to make the daybed, Susan handed him a pair of oversized floppy PJs that she had recovered from her dad's closet. She was wearing a similar pair, almost matched, but they were of a different color. Although James didn't sleep in the PJs, he smiled and thanked her.

The two sat on the bed, discussing the plan to go to the old house the next day. Susan was anxious and wanted to figure out everything that could set Rosemary free. As they were talking, James tenderly reached out and pulled Susan close. He tried to reassure her that everything would be alright. He also laughed and expressed how sexy she looked with her big Pajamas on.

Susan jumped up on the bed and hit him with the pillow. James was laughing, but he didn't try to stop her. Susan lost her balance and fell into his arms. He gently held her close for a moment, then picked her up and tucked her in before saying good night.

The following day, they got up early, showered, and got ready. They had a cup of coffee together as they discussed their plans for the day. "I'll pack picnic lunch; we'll share it under the big oak tree," Susan said gently.

As they were driving over to the property, Susan felt the pull of gravity, as she had felt before. This time, the energy felt different from Rosemary — it felt more powerful. As Susan tried to resist, she thought she heard Rosemary's voice, *"Be careful!"*

She was telling her to be careful. That was the first time she had heard from Rosemary in a long time, and she knew she was leading her to the house. Moreover, she still had not told anyone about being followed by a four-year-old kid, fearing they would laugh at her.

They arrived at the house and went inside. "There is no cat, Susan," James yelled as he was upstairs looking for clues. Susan noticed a door to the right. She opened it and went inside. "Hmm. Let's see what's in here," she pushed her hair back and started looking around. There was a small, rusted cast iron bed in the corner. As she was wandering around, she noticed a shadow following her.

"Is someone here?" She asked loudly. The restlessness in her voice was evident.

"*Yes, lovely,*" this time, she got a reply. "Did Rosemary send you?" the soft voice asked.

"I think she did, and I'm trying to help her reach the light," Susan replied.

"*We are all here, and Rosemary refuses to follow her destiny until we are all free.*"

The soft voice told Susan.

"What do you mean by *all?* Who are you?" Susan asked, but this time, there was no response.

A mysterious voice spoke to her as Susan found herself standing in a dark room. While she wasn't sure what to make out of it, she felt closer to Rosemary than ever.

"What can I do to help you reach the light?" Susan hoped Rosemary would answer her this time.

Chapter Seven

The Hunt

The encounter with spirits left Susan stunned. She stood there still, trying to grasp everything that had happened during the last few hours. When she didn't respond to any of his calls, James came to the room.

"Are you okay?" He rushed toward her when he saw her standing inside the room with a look of utter shock on her face.

"It's weird. I think..." Susan's voice broke as she tried to speak. "I heard some voices. And they were talking to me," she told James, looking around the room to find evidence to support her words.

"Voices? Are you sure?" James looked around the room. He got worried too. "I checked the house; there is no one here," he told Susan.

Susan started thinking about what she had heard earlier. It was clear that the spirits were speaking directly to her, and they wanted her to help them reach the light. However, she wasn't sure how to do that. She had still not heard from the clairvoyant from whom she bought the tarot cards. What was supposed to be a fun card game to keep her busy during lonely nights turned into an adventurous quest that kept her mind spinning.

With no news from the clairvoyant, Susan decided to consult with a priest from the old school. She told James about her decision after she told him that it might've been Rosemary's family who communicated with her.

Since Susan didn't know her way around town, James told her that he knew an elder of the church and they could talk to him about her encounter with the spirits. Susan was surprised that James agreed with her. At first, she thought he might not even believe her, but then he had been very supportive of her during this whole quest. He had become her strength while she was trying to figure out what had happened to Rosemary.

James and Susan took off from Rosemary's house in his truck and went to meet the elder. They finally arrived at what looked like a seminary. They entered a big auditorium with a giant belt hanging on the front of the wall. James walked over and pulled the cord to let someone know they were there.

When there was no response, he spoke a bit loudly. "Hello. Is anyone there?"

Susan was standing at a distance; her eyes wandered around the spacious room that was lit up with candles. Her mind kept wandering off to the encounter at Rosemary's house. She felt as if she was dreaming, and despite the fun she had at first with this adventure, she now only wanted the nightmare to end. But it wasn't a nightmare. It was all so real. No matter how many times she tried to think of it as a bad dream that would end once she woke up, she found herself investigating a case that happened at least 85 years ago.

While Susan was lost in her thoughts, an elder came into the room, and James asked to see John Paul, who used to reside there. The elder told James that John had died a couple of years ago.

"He was a great teacher and a source of help and wisdom. We shall miss him greatly," he added.

The elder further shared that John Paul was working with one of the younger priests on exorcism during his last days.

"Charleston," he revealed the name of John Paul's protégé and said he knew how to reach the light.

Susan and James looked at each other before they followed the elder into the office. Charleston greeted them warmly after James introduced him as a friend of John Paul. He heard their story with patience and was willing to help them solve the case. Charleston offered to meet them the following day at Rosemary's house at the decided time.

It was a relief for Susan and James. The two went back to Susan's place, ate leftovers, and then kicked back to watch a movie on TV. Their day was full of adventures, and they were tired from it. It didn't take them long to fall asleep.

The following day, they woke up on the couch with the TV still going on.

"Oh, no!" Susan yelled when she looked at her watch. They had to be at Rosemary's house in an hour to meet Charleston. Her voice startled James awake, who was still sleeping on the couch.

They both got up, washed their faces, and headed toward Rosemary's house, where Charleston was already waiting for them outside.

Susan got out of the truck and started walking toward Charleston. He was standing right in front of the house, observing every inch of it closely. This whole experience was also new to him. So far, Charleston had only read about demonic energy but had never witnessed it.

The sun was shining on top of them as they stood outside Rosemary's house, where everything looked normal, but Susan knew differently. She could sense a disturbance but wasn't sure what it was about or where it was coming from.

By this time, James had also gotten out of the truck and joined them. As soon as Susan began to take a step closer to the house, the priest grabbed her and pushed her back.

"Sorry, Susan. The house is surrounded by an electrical force that can be lethal. I have already called the electrical company to shut it down in the surrounding areas. It shouldn't take long."

As Susan tried to take another step back, she was jolted forward by force. It left her startled; James and Charleston seemed puzzled too.

"Are you okay?" James came forward and helped Susan stand straight. The next moment, a bright flash of light blinded their vision before a cloud of smoke covered the top of the house.

Susan, James, and Charleston looked at one another. They were prepared to face the encounter with the spirits. Charleston started mumbling something with his eyes closed and his cross close to his heart. Susan assumed he was reciting Bible verses. Before she could ask him, a voice echoed amidst the silence.

"Hello, Susan."

"Who is it?" Susan replied hesitantly. She was constantly looking all around her to see a face.

"It's me, Ben," the manly voice replied.

Susan had her speculations about who killed Rosemary, and Ben was the last person she expected to talk to during her spirit encounters. She wondered what he was doing at Rosemary's house.

The electrical energy started dissipating, and the cloud of smoke began to fade away. Charleston knew he had to act quickly so the spirit could reach the light.

"Did you kill Rosemary?" Charleston asked.

"No, of course not. I loved her," Ben replied.

"What are you doing at Rosemary's house?" Charleston asked the next question.

There was a pause for a few moments before Ben shared what happened to him after Rosemary's death.

"Before I went to college, I confronted him, but it was already too late. I finally found peace with myself and finished school. I taught in college and talked in seminars. Most of the money went to Ms. V for The Mission House and John and Tanya for the baby. I chose to do this for Rosemary."

Susan got teary-eyed listening to the story of his life. Ben truly loved Rosemary, and even after she died, he continued loving her by looking after her family, especially her mother.

"Who killed Rosemary?" Charleston asked him again.

"Tom did," the answer was brief this time.

"What are you doing here?" This time it was Susan who asked the question.

"I'm protecting the family from Tom," Ben replied.

While Charleston was speaking to Ben, Susan noticed a cloud breaking above the house. From there appeared a young woman dressed in white. Her skin was glowing, and her hair bounced as she floated down the cloud. She looked at Susan and nodded her head to thank her, and smiled. It was the first time Susan was looking at this young woman, but she knew it was Rosemary — the friend she found in loneliness and who needed her help.

Susan knew that Rosemary was there to take Ben with her. Together, the eternal lovers had to reach the light. Susan stepped forward and looked at the cloud. She smiled back at Rosemary before she turned to Ben.

"Ben, Rosemary thanks you for your sacrifice, and she loves you too. You will be relieved to know that she is standing above you in the light. She is waiting for you," Susan told Ben.

A loud thunder was heard, and Susan knew they were running out of time. This time, Charleston guided Ben toward Rosemary, where his light awaited him.

"I can see her," Ben replied as he saw the light above him.

Rosemary reached out and took his hand; they disappeared like a raindrop after falling on the ground.

Susan and James were amazed to witness the event they'd been working for this whole time. They had helped Rosemary and Ben reach the light and set their souls free. It was a miracle, indeed.

However, Susan knew that the job wasn't done. After the cloud of smoke disappeared, Susan, James, and Charleston went inside the house. There were other ghosts in the house who needed to be helped to see their lights. They wasted no time and decided to go in and direct them.

"Hello, miss. Your battle is over. You are going to join your family. Do you see the light?" Susan asked.

"Yes, Susan. We all see the light. We can never thank you enough for what you did. You are a gifted young lady," the voice stated.

Susan felt relieved. She stood there smiling as Charleston directed the spirits to the light. When the ceremony ended, Susan fell to her knees; sweat beads rolling down her skin. She felt as if a weight had been lifted off her chest.

James walked toward her and pulled her up. He was the only one who could understand how emotionally distorted she had been lately. He knew how relieved she must be after helping Rosemary's family reach the light.

"Let's go home," he said before he turned to Charleston. They both expressed gratitude to the priest for setting those trapped souls free. As a priest, Charleston was excited, for it was the first time he had a chance to witness such an event. He was living the hypothesis about where the energy came from in a demonic situation.

"Susan, don't be surprised if you receive other visitors some-day," he warned Susan in a humorous way. He sensed that Susan was blessed and she had the ability to comprehend beyond the seeming reality. Perhaps, it was her empathetic heart or kind soul that made her capable of conversing with the spirits.

"I don't think so," Susan laughed.

She then got into the truck with James and went home. As they drove home, several thoughts rushed to her mind. Now that Susan had solved the case of Rosemary, she wanted to focus on the farmhouse before leaving for home. She told James that she needed to fix the farm so that they would be self-sustained if necessary. James laughed when Susan complained that he still hadn't installed the elec-tric dishwasher.

"We could get that done soon, Susan," he replied while smiling.

They were both relieved to solve the mysterious case of *who killed Rosemary?* Now that they had no more mysteries to solve, they had a heart- to-heart conversation about life and how they felt in each other's company. They both enjoyed the conversation and didn't even realize it when they reached home. "Well, Susan, I'm going to spend one more night with you to ensure you are okay," James told Susan.

"I am okay. Trust me. I'll be fine," Susan reassured James as she got out of the car.

"Does that mean I need to go home?" James asked.

Susan pulled James closer and told him she needed to be alone tonight.

"You have been my strength. I couldn't have done this all without you. I just need some time to myself," Susan told James.

After James left, Susan felt a little lost. Though she was happy that Rosemary had finally reached the light, she felt like a part of her was missing. Knowingly or unknowingly, she enjoyed exploring the case that happened about 85 years ago.

Susan made a coffee for herself and went inside her father's office. She dragged the chair and rested her elbows on the wooden table. Right in front of her lay the box of tarot cards and the fan. She took a moment to think before she grabbed the tarot cards and laid them on the table.

"Let's begin!"

Chapter Eight

The Connection

Susan felt enlightened; as she rested, she restored her ability to comprehend what had happened to her. She needed time to analyze everything that had happened during the last few days, especially the encounter with Rosemary.

Remembering her childhood, she recalled experiencing dreams and visions. However, whenever she tried to talk to her mom about it, the answer was the same. *It was just a dream!*

However, after her encounter with Rosemary and the other spirits, she got to learn the meaning behind her visions and dreams. She couldn't help but think about all the visions she had seen since childhood. Accidents and deaths would not have happened if only someone had taken her seriously.

Growing up, Susan was always at the right place at the right time. The earliest remembrance she had of such incidents was at the camp where a young girl jumped off the dock and couldn't swim that well. As she was fighting for her life, the girl chose Susan to latch onto, despite others being closer. Susan didn't let her go and managed to swim underwater, with the girl holding the tide on top of her until they reached shallow water. Susan took her to safety and made sure she was alright. The girl thanked Susan as tears rolled down her cheeks.

"You are welcome," Susan said politely to the poor girl who was traumatized from the fear of drowning.

Susan recalled another incident when she was shopping in a big department store. While she was busy checking items off her grocery list, her aunt came. At first, Susan didn't recognize who it was, but her aunt identified her. Susan smiled as she saw her approaching her, but something was off. Her aunt looked pale and exhausted.

"Susan, what's happening to me?" she asked Susan.

Susan took her hand and tried to comfort her. But she sensed something different.

"It looks like you are having a stroke," words came out of Susan's mouth all of a sudden.

Susan immediately took her to the nearest hospital, where the doctors gave her the initial treatment. Susan was relieved when she saw her in recovery. She still had no idea how she ended up saving her life in the end.

All these years, Susan shrugged off these incidences, thinking of them as coincidences. However, now that she thought about it, there were far too many incidents to be coincidences. Susan was beginning to recognize her ability to help and heal people. She had possessed this power all along, but only now had she realized her true potential. Perhaps, that was one of the reasons why her law firm was so successful.

It was a bitter-sweet feeling. As Susan was preparing to leave, she started getting worried that James would never call or check on her again. She promised herself not to cave and tell him all the stories, as she planned to meet him later that day.

In the evening, Susan decided to walk out in the yard and stumbled over a stump. The moment she fell to the ground, she saw a big black hole in front of her and thought she saw someone inside it. For a moment, Susan was stunned; she wondered how she had ended up in front of the dark hole. *Who was it?* She thought it was a man who needed her help.

It all happened in a matter of seconds, and then the black hole disappeared. Susan was hurt; she struggled to get up and walk to the rose garden. Once there, she took a deep breath, letting herself soak in the fragrance of flowers.

After feeling better and checking herself for any injuries, she got into her car and went to check on James. When she arrived at his house, everything was locked up, with no sign of James. She got worried and started calling out his name as she walked the property at a distance.

It was getting dark. All of a sudden, she heard a strange sound; it was like someone was rubbing two metals against each other. Susan decided to follow the sound. It was James, who was covered in dirt from head to toe, looking like a caveman. He was inside a dark hole and in dire need of help. It was exactly like the vision Susan had seen earlier that day.

"Oh, no. Are you alright, James?" Susan yelled, hoping her voice would reach him.

"I was working in the backyard when I accidentally fell," James told her as his voice broke.

Susan immediately called the fire department and an ambulance to rescue him. Meanwhile, she kept reassuring James that help was on the way. Thankfully, the rescue service was there quickly; they didn't waste any moment pulling James out cautiously. The ambulance carried James to the hospital to get him checked out, and Susan followed. James smiled and pulled her close as he whispered, "Thank you, Susan."

Susan smiled and reassured him again that it was going to be alright. She ran her fingers through his hair, that were covered in dirt.

"You go home, and I will call you when I'm about to be released," James told her. He didn't want her to go through any more trouble for him. He was grateful that she had saved his life.

Although Susan didn't like leaving him alone, she kissed him on the cheek and left. She stopped and picked up a few things to prepare dinner at home. All this time, she could not stop thinking about James. She hoped he would be released from the hospital and join her for dinner.

Little did she know James was going to be released soon, but he didn't want Susan to know because he was planning a surprise for her.

***

After James was released from the hospital, he drove into town to visit the jewelry store. He looked at many rings but kept going back to one. His eyes were set on a beautiful 14-karat gold ring embellished with a flawless diamond with a few small diamonds on each side. James knew that he would have to sell a few shares of stock to buy that ring, but he knew Susan was worth it.

"I'll take this one," James told the store clerk.

After getting the ring, James called Susan to inform her that he would visit her later that evening. He was so happy that he couldn't stop smiling. He went home, showered, and got dressed for the special occasion. He had decided to propose to Susan that day and wanted to make it as special as possible.

Susan was relieved that James was doing better now and looked forward to meeting him. She prepared their favorite meal, steak, potatoes, and salad, and put on her black dress and diamond necklace. She wanted to look gorgeous as this would be their first official date as a couple.

It was 10 already, but James had still not arrived. Susan got worried as it was getting dark, and she decided to call him. As soon as she dialed his number, she heard a knock at the door. She ran toward the door and was relieved to see James standing there.

"Oh, my goodness. You look gorgeous!" James exclaimed the moment Susan opened the door and greeted him.

"Thank you," Susan blushed as she held the door open for him to enter. "I'm glad you are okay," she added with a smile. She decided not to tell him about her falling in the garden, knowing he would get worried. Moreover, she didn't want him to worry too much about her as she had all these realistic visions lately. That night, she wanted it to be just about her and James.

James brought the steaks off the grill, and Susan poured her favorite wine and lit the candles. They ended up creating a beautiful setting for a cozy, candlelight dinner. Susan didn't notice as James dropped the ring in her wine glass. As he watched Susan pick her wine glass up, he proposed a toast, "To us, Susan."

"To us, James," Susan said as she raised her wine glass in the air. That's when it made a clicking sound, and Susan noticed the beautiful diamond ring at the bottom of her glass.

"Oh, my God!" she couldn't help but exclaim loudly.

As James started to sip wine, Susan smiled at him. She downed her wine in one long gulp and took the ring out of the glass. James took the ring from her hand and knelt down to propose to her.

Susan was speechless. It was a new beginning for both of them. Before this, they had never expressed their love for one another, but they knew they had a special connection.

The evening turned dreamy as Susan and James talked and laughed together. Susan also shared her plans for the farmhouse before leaving for the city.

She decided to go on a trip to visit her children, who were entirely too busy in their lives. She was sure that they would be ecstatic about the news. Susan was excited and asked James if he would like to join her on the road trip and meet her children. At first, James was hesitant and nervous because he wanted her children to like him and didn't want to risk it all in haste.

Susan expressed the need to visit the firm to check on her employees and learn about the cases they were handling.

Eventually, James agreed to go on the road trip but told Susan that he had to take care of some business that would take a couple of days.

Meanwhile, Susan thought everything through. She, too, wanted her children to get along with James. She realized it would be less awkward if the children came home for dinner and met James.

As they continued having dinner, Susan told James about her plans. The house was on the beach, where James could fish or bathe in the sun. "That sounds like a plan!" James chuckled.

Susan called her children and let them know she would be visiting the company she had worked so hard to build. Both children said they would try to make it in. Meanwhile, James and Susan were enthusiastic about their first trip together. They hoped to have some good family time with everyone.

***

The week went by quickly. Susan and James packed their stuff and were ready to hit the road. Once again, Susan found herself lost in the beauty of the magnificent Mississippi River as they drove on the Great River Road. She couldn't help but think about Rosemary, buried inside this untamed river. When Susan was driving to the farmhouse, she was alone. However, this time James was accompanying her, and it made her journey less painstaking.

The journey took about eight hours, and they finally arrived at the beach house. James was astounded by the beauty of the ocean and the house. It was serene and calm, yet breathtaking. It reminded him of Susan. Beautiful and *caring!*

Susan gave a house tour to James, and then they walked out by the beachside.

"It's gorgeous here, Susan," James said when he couldn't keep his eyes off the ocean.

"It must be a significant change for you," Susan was worried about James and wanted to make sure he was doing alright in the new place.

"I love it here!" he exclaimed.

"I haven't been able to sort things out ever since my husband died,"

Susan's smile faded as she said those words. "Perhaps we could do it together. It's just something to think about," she added quickly.

"Oh, I would love to," James once again showed full support for her plan. Susan smiled.

Later, Susan visited her office and surprised everyone. They looked overwhelmed, drowning in paperwork. Now that Susan had arrived, they were relieved, knowing how good she was at managing things. Finally, Eric came in, grabbed her by the arm, and took her to his office.

Eric was her secretary, a second-year law student with a brilliant mind, and Susan trusted him.

"It looks like everyone is on overload," Susan remarked.

She then asked Eric what she could do to help straighten things out. She learned that Eric wasn't aiming to graduate with honors, and she thought he was ready to take the junior executive position and have him on staff.

Eric refused the offer because he didn't want to upset others who had been there longer. Susan understood and asked him to plan a morning meeting with all her staff. She wanted to hear their concerns and figure out what she could do to make things better.

After Susan returned to the beach house, she spent a wonderful evening at the beach with James. They really enjoyed each other's company and had a great time. They even went to a beach party.

The evening turned out to be great, but both of them were exhausted. Susan politely offered James the guest room before she went to her bedroom. "Good night," James said as he kissed her on the cheeks.

When Susan stepped inside her bedroom, she felt something was different. She opened the window to feel the ocean breeze and listen to the waves. Her mind was swarming with so many thoughts as she lay on the bed with her eyes open. She was shocked when a familiar voice broke into her ears right before she was about to doze off.

Susan immediately got up and looked around. Near the window, she thought she saw a bright tornado of light, and the voice was coming from it. It sounded like her husband. She got up the next moment and walked toward the window. Tears of joy started rolling down her eyes. She was finally able to connect with her late husband and help him reach his life.

"Joe, is that you?" her voice broke as she asked.

"Yes, Susan. It's me," Joe's voice echoed.

Susan felt as if her body was a magnet to dead. Joe told Susan he had been wandering around, totally lost in darkness. Susan felt as if their minds were connected.

"Look up, Joe, and close your eyes. Do you see the light? I have forgiven you for all of your mistakes, but you must forgive yourself, too," she said politely, knowing that her husband was listening to her.

"Your family is doing great and loves you deeply. But you need to follow the light...." Before she could say anything else, the light started to fade.

"Thank you, Susan," his voice echoed before it faded entirely.

Susan felt at peace after a long time. Knowing that her husband had now reached his light, she could rest, knowing a huge burden had been taken off her chest. That night, she slept like a baby.

The following day, Susan jumped out of bed. She knew she had a lot to do that day. She had an important meeting at the firm, and her children were coming in the evening. As Susan was getting late, she just made a cup of coffee for herself and rushed out the door. She didn't want to wake James up, so she decided to leave quietly.

When James eventually got up, he knew Susan had left. He got into the kitchen and started making breakfast. That's when a beautiful young lady opened the door and entered to find him in the kitchen. It was Anna, Susan's daughter.

"Something smells good," Anna said.

"Then you are just in time, Anna," James recognized her as Susan had already told him about her.

Anna was taken aback to see a stranger cooking breakfast in her mother's house and knowing her name. "Who are you?" she was intrigued and asked with a smile.

"I'm James. I'm your mother's friend from Mississippi. I'm helping her renovate the farmhouse," James introduced himself.

"Nice meeting you," Anna smiled and replied.

"It appears your mother left early for a meeting with her firm," James then told her.

"That sounds like mom. She takes her job very seriously," Anna remarked as she laughed.

James smiled as he was aware of how passionate Susan was about everything she did. As the two continued talking, they were joined by Derek, Anna's brother. He, too, was intrigued to meet James, who added another plate for him.

Together with Derek and Anna, James enjoyed the breakfast. It gave him the opportunity to connect with Susan's children as he wanted to be 'likable' in their eyes. Both the children were impressed by James right away as they talked to him about life in Mississippi and what James did for a living. They were captivated by his life story and enjoyed his company.

After having breakfast, Anna and Derek helped James clean the table. By the time James finished washing the dishes, Susan had walked in. Her children gave her a big hug and a lot of kisses.

"You are terrific, Mom," they reminded her how much they loved her.

Susan felt delighted to see her children again. She wanted to tell them about her encounter with Joe last night but decided to keep it to herself for now. Everything had turned out great so far, and Susan was relieved to see James getting along with Derek and Anna.

However, there was still one question that she was asking herself.

Is there anyone else waiting for me to reach the light?

Chapter Nine

Confession

Susan admitted that it had been a daunting experience. Before going to the beach house, she was unsure how her children would react to meeting James, but she wanted their first meeting to be perfect and memorable. Fortunately, everything turned out to be well, and after she saw her children and James getting along, she was happy and relieved. Susan thought her children loved James, and she couldn't help but talk about it on the way back.

On their way home from the beach house, Susan was thinking about how much her children had liked James, and he teased her about being jealous.

"I think you're a little jealous, Susan," he said. She couldn't help but smile because she knew he was right. The two chuckled as they talked about their time with the kids. Susan was glad it turned out to be a memorable trip for everyone.

As they were getting close to the house, the sky clouded up, and it appeared not a moment too soon. "How classic!" she thought.

When they arrived at the house, James walked Susan inside, looking around to make sure everything was intact. After their experience during the last few weeks, James had become highly protective of Susan and would always ensure she was doing okay. As everything was the same as they left, James felt satisfied and asked Susan if she was ready for kitchen renovations tomorrow or if she was too tired to do anything.

"I'm okay, James. I'll see you in the morning," she replied and hugged James before he left.

Although Susan was exhausted, she was also excited about everything happening in her life lately. She got ready for bed, and before she could reminisce about the past few days of her life, she fell asleep.

The next day, she woke up refreshed and energized and was ready for the day ahead. James walked in as she poured the coffee, and he seemed eager to get started on the kitchen renovations. James worked hard all day rebuilding the kitchen wall and replacing the windows in front of the sink. Susan was there all the time, helping him out. She admired his hard work and efforts; he was so involved in making the place better for Susan. The two had lunch together, and then in the evening, Susan prepared a quick snack for the two to have during work. "You are the best, Susan," James said as he took a big bite of the sandwich.

By 6 pm, the two finished all the work and looked around to admire their accomplishment. Susan couldn't believe her eyes as James finished with his magic touch. As she looked around her kitchen, Susan couldn't help but admire James' handiwork — he had turned the place around. She was thinking about what else they could do to the place, but James had other plans.

He kept staring at Susan, smiling the entire time. He then asked Susan to sit down because he wanted to set a date for the wedding. He sounded pretty serious when he said that. Susan's eyes opened wide because it came as a shock to her. At the same time, she felt happy to be loved by such an amazing guy.

Susan sat by James as he looked at her. He took her hand in his and looked deep into her eyes before whispering, "I love you. I love you, Susan, and I want to marry you now, with or without a big fat wedding."

"Now?" Susan was uncertain about the rush, but it made sense because all their friends and family were busy. Susan thought about her children and wondered if they could make time for her wedding. Given how busy they were, she decided not to trouble them by asking them to come there all the way. She discussed all of that with James, and by the end of their conversation, she didn't want a big fat wedding either. She agreed that the idea of a rushed wedding was much better.

"Okay, James. But can we manage everything on our own?" she asked James. "You don't have to worry about anything. I'll handle it," James smiled as he held her hand tightly.

It was decided that they would get their marriage license and make the appointment right away. They both freshened up and went into town to get their license. While in town, Susan looked around different shops to find a necklace. She found a good piece in one of the shops that James bought her. She got a pair of socks for James as well.

They also met the clerk, who told them they had an appointment available for her at 4 pm the next day, and she agreed. Before returning home, James suggested they stop for dinner in town. Throughout the dinner, the two were busy chatting and laughing. They had a good time together, and James expressed that Susan made him "the luckiest man in the city!"

The next day, Susan was up bright and early. She was so excited about the big day that she kept smiling as she packed a small bag for her. When she walked down the stairs, the smell of bacon was fine, so she knew breakfast was almost ready. Susan prepared their coffee as James fixed her plate. After breakfast, James went home to get ready for the wedding.

Meanwhile, Susan decided to walk outside. She enjoyed seeing beautiful flowers blooming under the sun and the sound of leaves crackling underneath her feet; she was enjoying nature's breathtaking symphony. She felt calm and serene as she walked the path and admired her colorful garden. She reflected on the chaos-filled city life where she used to remain constantly busy. Here, she felt peaceful. While she was great at her work, she felt a sense of belonging here, in this house, and with James.

Susan lost track of time and finally went upstairs and started to get ready for the evening. She looked absolutely breathtaking in a simple white dress with diamonds on her fingers and the beautiful necklace from James around her neck. She saw her reflection in the mirror and couldn't help but smile. That's when she heard the sound of a horn; it appeared James had arrived.

Susan was walking down the stairs when James walked in through the door and saw her on the stairs. He was speechless for a few moments but eventually composed himself enough to utter, "You look stunning!"

James took Susan's bag, and they rushed out the door. They arrived at the courthouse just in time to meet the clerk. They had to go down the stairs to enter the judge's office with a license in hand. When the judge asked about the witnesses, Susan's children walked in.

Susan was surprised, and she smiled. Anna pointed toward James as he was the one who told them to come. James knew how much Susan loved her children, and he wanted to surprise her. The small ceremony commenced, and the words echoed amidst the silence, *"Now I pronounce you husband and wife. You may kiss the bride."*

Susan blushed as James kissed her. She thought life couldn't be any more incredible now that she was with her family, including James. Her children had to catch a plane soon, so they didn't have much time to celebrate. But they ended up taking a family picture together.

James had asked them if they had time for dinner. "No way," Anna replied. "We are okay. We have a rental, and you two have to be on your way to the honeymoon," she wanted the newlywed couple to have some time alone. James told Anna and Eric that he would pay for them to fly whenever they wanted to visit. The children appreciated his gesture and hugged him before they left.

James then looked at his bride; he had a surprise ready for Susan when they left the court. "We are going on a road trip to the city, a casino," he told her before they got into the jeep and started their journey.

As they drove to Mississippi City, every street lit up with bright lights. They entered a huge parking lot, and as they parked the car, a young man arrived and took their bags. He asked Susan and James to follow him to the banquet room. The moment Susan entered the banquet room, the lights were turned on, and family and friends were waiting for the couple to arrive.

"Surprise!" the crowd roared.

Susan looked at James with surprise and love in her eyes. The song started playing as James pulled Susan to the dance floor. While they moved to the beat of the music, James told her that he owned a private jet, and Anna invited all of Susan's friends. She was pleasantly surprised because the evening was going way better than Susan had planned. She thought it would be an evening to remember for a long time.

Just before dawn, everyone retired to the rooms to sleep for a while. They met again for breakfast, where Susan stood at the table, proposed a toast, and thanked her children and friends for making her wedding memorable. After everyone left, James and Susan went home to start a new journey together. It was an unusual feeling; they both couldn't believe they were married.

The next morning, Susan told James she was going outside to water the flowers and that he could put the coffee on. Walking down the pathway leading to the flowers, she felt like someone was watching her. It was like Déjà vu, and she was stunned for a minute. Susan heard the leaves rustling behind her as she sat on the bench James had placed in the middle of the garden.

"I know you're here," Susan said calmly. The movement stopped, and silence around her grew as she remained seated on the bench without losing her nerves. The next moment, she turned and froze in fear as a giant snake appeared out of nowhere, slithered over, and wrapped itself around her tightly. She felt suffocated and found it hard even to breathe. Susan tried to remain calm as she asked the demon why it wanted to frighten her.

"Oh, YOU are scared?" the demon said, *"I've been scared for a long time."*

Throughout her unusual experiences, if Susan had learned one thing, it was to stay calm. The snake kept growing taller and taller while tightening its grip around her. Its jaws were wide with overlapping fangs. His mouth and red tongues slithered in and out. The snake's voice was deep and scratchy.

"What do you want from me? Is it about Rosemary?" Susan asked.

"I want justice. I had an entire village condemn me for Rosemary's death. I must prove my innocence to reach the light of the Holy world." Susan recognized who the demon was right away. It was Tom.

Susan wondered what it was that he needed to tell her. *"When I met Tanya, she took my breath away with her beauty and energy,"* Tom continued, *"After gaining her trust, I fell in love with her."*

He vented.

"Susan, you are the woman of light," the slippery demon or Tom spoke powerfully as now Susan had come to realize. He told Susan he was a friend and didn't want to harm her in any way, but he didn't have a choice in how he appeared in front of Susan.

It was shocking for Susan as she sat there alone, trying hard to breathe, making sense of everything the demon was telling her. That's when James opened the door and yelled for her.

"Susan, coffee is ready," he said.

The snake disappeared into thin air when Susan heard James' voice. She looked around and wondered if it was a reality or a bad dream she had seen in broad daylight.

Chapter Ten

Deep Under

It had been months since Susan had an encounter with Tom. It took Susan a long time to comprehend what she had witnessed that day.

"Was it real? Did I somehow end up in a different world? What did Tom want from me?"

Several questions in her mind were fading away against the race of time. She wondered if Tom had sorted out his dilemma independently and reached his light. "I am free!" Susan shouted as she was dusting the flight of stairs.

Although James knew something was up when he saw her troubled, Susan decided not to tell him anything. Her encounter with a giant snake had kept her restless for weeks, but all she wanted was to be at peace, and that's what she was working on.

Her life had witnessed a massive change. Getting married to James was the right decision, and she felt happy to be able to enjoy this new journey of her life with the man she loved. Her mind was lost in the joyful memories the two had made together in the last few months, and she couldn't help but smile. That's when James walked into the house; he looked as excited and bright as ever.

"Hey Susan, would you like to go out to the boat today?" he asked as he tossed her coat onto the sofa.

"Sounds like a plan!" Susan replied with equal enthusiasm. She took two steps at a time to reach him where he stood at the bottom of the stairs and let him catch her in his embrace.

"I'll get started then," James kissed her on the cheek before he made a quick run to the garage and got his fishing tackle and tools. Then he made his way out to the truck.

Susan went to the bedroom and got dressed. She wore a bright yellow dress with a hat and let her hair fall down past her shoulders. She then picked up the bag and went to the kitchen to get the cooler.

Meanwhile, James went out and booked a boat for the two of them. Once he got off the call, he started blowing the truck horn as Susan locked the door and made her way into the truck.

"Let's go," she said as she sat beside James.

It was a bright, sunny day; the weather was pleasantly warmer than they expected. Susan took a deep breath as she enjoyed the warmth of the sun kissing her skin.

"Someone looks happy," James remarked as he pinched her cheek. Susan laughed and asked James how long it would take.

"We are almost there," James said as they drove down the tiny dirt road surrounded by a swamp, huge trees, and brush. He drove a few miles to an open clearing with a boat ramp. Finally, they reached the riverside, where James had booked a boat for them.

"Yay!!!" Susan shouted as he got out of the truck and jumped into the boat. James smiled as he took the stuff out of the truck and started trolling down the river.

As James was busy setting up his fishing rod, Susan sat there admiring the beautiful view of nature in its purest form. She felt the beauty of the translucent colors of the river and the gentle breeze touching her face. She could feel there was so much more to this beautiful spring than met the eye.

She didn't know much about fishing, but she was excited to be there with James. Closely observing as James threw his line in the water, she hoped he would catch a big fish. She was cheering him on the entire time and taking pictures simultaneously as it turned out to be a memorable day.

In the distance, Susan looked at the vibrant flowers lining up the sides of the river; they were romantic and aerial, almost angelic. Susan felt herself almost falling into a trance because she was so relaxed.

However, nothing seemed to bother James because he was just enjoying his fishing time. "Oh wow. That's a big one," he exclaimed after he managed to catch a big fish.

Susan jumped up excitedly and almost ended up falling out of the boat. Thanks to James, who was sitting right next to her, she got her footing back. He just laughed as she grabbed him and exclaimed, "So you think that's funny?"

James could not stop laughing at her, and even Susan herself laughed so hard that tears filled her eyes and ran down her cheeks as she tried to contain herself. James calmly put Susan on the seat and put the fish in the cooler. He then pulled a bottle of wine from the cooler and poured it into two glasses.

"To us and our love!" he raised his glass in the air before he sat down by her side. Susan lay her head on his shoulder and held his hand tightly. The two of them sat there for a few minutes, embracing the love they had for each other and smiling their hearts out. The two would always feel happy in each other's presence, and ever since they got married, they just could not get enough of each other.

After a while, James turned to his fishing again while Susan drank her wine. She was happy and relaxed after a long time and wanted this day to last forever. Little did she know that what was coming next would scare her to death.

As Susan was sitting at the back of the boat, she heard scratching underneath it. "What is it?" she asked.

"What is what, Susan?" James seemed clueless.

"The noise," Susan replied as she could still hear the noise.

James shook his head and acted like he didn't hear a thing. At first, Susan thought he was messing with her, but when he remained clueless, she knew it was only her. She could still hear it, and it was getting louder with each passing second, almost hurting her eardrums. It was like Déjà vu; she knew it would not take long before the circumstances became intense. She had to do something now as she didn't want herself to be trapped in the dark world again. She yelled at James to help her from drowning into the darkness that was slowly taking over her vision, but there was no response from his side.

It was like she was transcending into some kind of a parallel world because James couldn't hear her voice or see her. Slowly, the darkness took over her vision, and the next moment, she was in a dark cave. Susan was scared as she found herself in this gigantic underworld where she saw the giant snake again — *Tom!*

She could see the snake in the distance, slowly creeping toward her. At the same time, Susan could hear Tom's voice as if he was talking to her, but she couldn't understand what he was saying. "What is going on?" she yelled, hoping her voice would reach Tom.

"On your right side, Susan. Run!" Tom told her as the snake was creeping toward her from the left.

While Tom tried to guide her, Susan did her best to find a way to escape, but her efforts were in vain. The more distance she covered, the more demons she encountered in the dark world. Susan got scared as all of these demons were getting restless.

Tom once again appeared in the form of a snake and was trying to reach out to Susan to help her find a way, but the other demons of the dark world were crawling all over her. Susan tried to scramble around the body of a snake, but it was too slippery, and she fell down after losing her grip. She was trying to talk to Tom but had no luck.

A loud scream was heard in the background, and Susan was not sure who it was, but it was terrifying.

"Tom," Susan yelled shortly after the scream. She felt something slithering around her, making her itchy in the skin. Susan stood up to see the snake standing right in front of her.

"We have 10 minutes to leave this place before the door closes," Tom told Susan; his deadly red eyes looked right through her, sending shivers down her spine. Since Susan had no other choice, she just followed Tom's instructions, hoping she would find a way out of this

dark realm. Suddenly, everything turned quiet, and within seconds, they returned to the bank of the river, where Susan and James arrived in their truck. When she looked around, she found no trace of James.

"He must be terrified by now," she started crying and wished he had never got involved with Rosemary's story. Beautiful memories of them together came rushing to her head as the last thing she wanted in her life was to lose James.

"It appears all of you are terrible demons, and none of you cares about me," Susan yelled as she could not stop crying. She was worried about James and wondered if he was also stuck in the dark underground world like her.

After Susan managed to escape the dark world, she went on to sit on the log on a riverbank with a massive snake inside her, filling her guts and sitting next to her at the same time. It was like the snake was a part of her, but still, she could see him beside her. Susan felt weak and nauseous and had no idea what to do. There was no person in sight to help her out. As Susan gasped for air and cried in hopelessness, the gate of heaven opened up. From there, she could see angels in a beautiful field surrounding her. It was like she was dreaming, but at least it did not appear to be a nightmare this time. One angel came forward and whispered to her. *"Susan, you have never been alone, and you are more loved than you will ever realize,"* the angel smiled at her before he went back up through the gate of heaven.

"Don't leave me," Susan screamed. She was still frightened because of her encounter with the massive snake in the underground world. Moreover, she was still not sure what her purpose was. She had this gift to see those who had departed from this world long ago; however, she was still not sure how to use it. It was like the answer was right in front of her, but something was stopping her from embracing her power.

That's when another angel appeared as she sat there with tears streaming down her face. Susan looked at the angel, and she recognized her. For a moment, she was stunned.

"Hello, Susan. It's me, Rosemary," the angel said. She was wearing a white dress that flew through her body elegantly, making her look as if she was floating amidst the clouds. Her hair was long and angelic; her voice soft and sweet.

"Oh my," Susan exclaimed. "I am glad you are okay! I missed you so much," Susan was happy to see Rosemary, and she started crying again.

"Look at the angels over there; that's my family. You saved them and reunited us. We owe it to you, Susan," Rosemary expressed her gratitude to Susan.

"Why me?" Susan only had one question.

"You are unique. You are one of the chosen angels who live on earth and help others to find the light," Rosemary told her.

Susan's tears started drying up, and her anger exploded as she reminded the angels that they had tossed her into the pits of hell. She was still worried about James and had no idea where to find him. She didn't know if he was even unharmed.

"So, where were you then when I needed help?" she asked angrily.

Rosemary entered the circle, "Look around you, Susan! The snake honking at your feelings and still sitting close by is called an 'attachment.' It attaches itself to the earth angels whenever it can and will appear in many demented ways to scare you, but it is powerless against the earth angels. You have the power to make it go away if you want to…."

Susan interrupted Rosemary and responded sharply, "It didn't seem too vulnerable when he took me to the devil's den!"

Rosemary laughed and replied, "That's because you were scared and uncertain, and that's why all of your friends are here teaching and showing you how to use your gift."

Susan had no idea what Rosemary was saying, and she sat there, staring at her cluelessly.

"Let me explain it to you, Susan. For instance, tell the snake to be gone, and it will disappear that very moment. Try it now. Go on," Rosemary added.

Susan took a deep breath before looking at the demon and, in a demanding voice, said, "Be gone!"

To her surprise, the snake disappeared without any resistance. A spark gleamed in Susan's hands as she had just seen a glimpse of her power.

Susan felt happy and relieved. She decided to return to the boat, where she could see James now, still fishing. All this time, Rosemary stayed with Susan, making sure she understood the power she possessed. That's when Rosemary told Susan the truth about Tom and why he wanted to connect to Susan.

"Tom saw his death long before the others and died from a heart attack. He was a good person who tried to help Tanya with her drug addiction. When he was at the river, he was there to meet me because he was worried about Tanya. He didn't realize that Tanya was clean from the day she realized she was pregnant. It was a twisted web of lies and deceit and had to unravel thread by thread. We couldn't have done it without you, Susan. We all thank you for helping us reach our light," Rosemary told Susan before she continued, "Now that you have understood, you can go live with James and not worry about a monster popping up beside you because you are protected and have all the power to help others when the occasion arises."

That's the last thing Rosemary said to Susan before she vanished into thin air. All her words spoken were the truth.

Chapter Eleven

Give Some Blessings

After her final encounter with Rosemary at the lake, Susan felt calm. It was a much-needed relief amidst the growing chaos. The experience did not only vanish her fears but also taught her how to use her powers to help troubled souls reach the light. She was an angel on earth, and she was now aware of the responsibility that came with her powers.

To others, her visions might sound like dreams, but Susan knew that her experiences were real. She had accepted that there was heaven and hell and ghosts and goblins who lived around her. She was at the center of many unknown entities, and while it was all too overwhelming, she believed that *life goes on!*

***

Summer is the best time to go fishing in Mississippi. As James had a great day at fishing, he decided to invite family and friends for a small lunch at the farmhouse. As Susan watched James clean up the fish and prepare them to fry, she could tell that he was no stranger when it came to cooking out.

In the yard, they had set up a grill; the smoky aroma had permeated the air. To accommodate the guests, James had several long fold tables, 25 to be exact. As he was busy at the grill, Susan didn't want to bother him, so she started unfolding the tables by herself. It had turned out to be a bright day, and she felt happy as she focused on aligning the tables. That's when a couple of James' friends showed up.

They looked about his age and equally enthusiastic about celebrating his *fishing adventure.* When they saw Susan setting up the tables by herself, they yelled from across the driveway, "No, Susan, we came to help with that."

"Oh, thank you so much. That's very kind of you," Susan appreciated their help and sighed in relief.

While James' friends got to work, Susan pulled out the beautiful white tablecloths and napkins she had kept for special occasions and set the tables. This was the first time the couple was hosting a luncheon at their house, and she wanted to make sure that everything was perfect.

She had an eye for decorating, and it was evident. Susan intricately created many beautiful designs with flowers as she arranged them on the tables with cutlery. She had hired a couple of servers to refresh the beverages and greeted them politely as she went on to overlook the arrangements.

After everything was done and settled, Susan stood back and looked at her beautiful arrangements. She couldn't help but smile as she had done a remarkable job. As her eyes were fixed on the table, James walked up to her. He couldn't believe his eyes.

"Susan, this is fantastic! You are amazing," he said as he came closer to kiss her.

"I'm glad you liked the arrangements. I have also checked on the catering and the servers; everything looks fine. I guess we are good to go," she told James, then asked, "Are you excited?" James could only nod as he was in awe of his talented wife. He got a little emotional as he realized how special she was.

Everything was in place when the guests arrived; Susan and James stood together and greeted all of them warmly.

As the gathering commenced, the day turned a whole lot livelier. Everyone was having a great time, enjoying the food and the company. Susan was talking to one of the guests when James interrupted as he stood up, tapping his wine glass to get everyone's attention.

"I don't know which one of you will get the only lucky fish I caught myself yesterday, but whoever it is, I'm sure they would pass it on to others. Thanks to all of you for coming and joining us on this pleasant evening. Cheers!" As usual, James won the hearts with a quirky comment as he went on to appreciate everyone who had come that evening.

Seeing the guests mingling and laughing made James and Susan excited that they had done something right. It was certainly a day to remember, and they all took several photographs to keep those moments locked as memories. After the guests had left and the servers had cleaned up, Susan and James returned home.

***

The new kitchen and the living room looked amazing, and Susan couldn't help but admire her remodeled house. The long glass windows gleamed the entire area surrounding the living room. All Susan needed now was the furniture that she had ordered. "It should be on its way," she thought as she recalled the ordered items. There was a couch, a wooden table, and a comfy leather chair that she had specifically ordered for James.

After a pleasantly busy day, Susan and James just relaxed; they laughed as they discussed the beautiful memories they had made at lunch.

As the day lingered, Susan reminded James that they had to take the horses for a ride. "It's time to put on our boots and a hat, get on the horses, and go for a ride," Susan suggested; she sounded excited as she pointed out that the weather seemed even more pleasant in the evening.

Although Susan was quite new to ranching and still learning her way around the farm, her support provided tremendous help to James in looking after everything. The two of them *cowboyed* up and drove to the ranch. Susan had already decided which horse she would ride. *"Velvet,"* she thought as she was excitedly looking forward to it, but she didn't say anything to James.

Surprisingly, when they reached the farm, James looked at Susan with a smirk and said, "Today, I am going to ride Velvet."

Susan looked at him and noticed his smile. James started laughing as he was only teasing Susan, knowing that Velvet was Susan's favorite.

"You love to do that, don't you?" Susan remarked as he lightly hit him on his hand. She was happy that she got to ride velvet.

"Ha-ha. I'm sorry. I just love to tease you," James responded as he entered the stables.

James and Susan got the horses ready and saddled up before they rode across acres of the ranch. As the two were enjoying the lovely evening weather, they also made sure to check up on the cows, deciding which ones James would take for auction the next day.

An idea entered Susan's mind when James talked about the auction. She thought it would be exciting to go to the auction with James the next day. She loved how he would always make her feel wanted and special by involving her in everything he did. "Can Velvet win against Leo?" James asked Susan sarcastically while patting his horse. He then looked at Susan before they went back to the ranch and started racing.

The day turned more adventurous for Susan; however, her beloved horse lost against Leo.

"That was fun," James said.

"You know Leo is faster than Velvet," Susan replied, exasperated, although she enjoyed the race.

In response, James just tilted his hat and nodded. He then rode into the stables and helped Susan get off the horse. As the beautiful sunset sprinkled glitters of gold in the surrounding, Susan and James decided to return home. The two of them had a lot of fun, and they laughed the entire walk back to the farmhouse.

Later that night, James looked at Susan, who seemed to be lost in her thoughts. He went ahead to sit next to her and asked, "Would you like to go on a cruise tomorrow?"

"I would think about it," Susan replied.

"Alright! I'll be waiting," James smiled as he patted her hand. He assumed she might be scared of the water and decided not to bug her.

Susan remained silent; something was troubling her. Once again, she found herself drifting away from reality and into the world of her dreams — the other side. She couldn't help but wonder how many more secrets were hidden in the world around her, especially in Mississippi. Ever since she arrived here, her life had become an adventure. And on this beautiful journey, she met James, who had promised to stick with her through thick and thin.

James got up from the sofa and picked up the morning paper. It had been a busy day, and he didn't even get time to read the headlines.

"Apparently, a dinner boat has crashed in the Mississippi River," he told Susan as he read the newspaper.

Susan's eyes got big when she heard the news. The flashbacks of Rosemary drowning in the river came back to her mind.

"We should go there and help," she suggested.

James was shocked. He just looked at Susan and replied, "The authorities are looking into this. I'm sure they can handle this."

Susan knew that it was not the right time to argue, so she just nodded.

She sat back and sipped her coffee. Seemingly, she was sitting in her living room, but in her mind, she was swimming in the dark waters of the Mississippi River, ready to uncover the secrets it held within its depth.

* 9 7 9 8 8 9 4 7 9 1 3 6 4 *